About the Author

Pete Mackley: A working-class, ordinary man. Born in Nottingham in 1960 but after a long and winding journey ended up in Cornwall, which has been home for the last twenty years.

I've worked for too many years in too many jobs, but the last twelve years have been in social care settings, homeless shelters, residential detox, residential rehab, prison and community services. I've worked alongside amazing colleagues and with incredible clients and this collection of experiences has been the inspiration for this book.

When I told my children I was thinking about writing a book, and what the subject was, they said it sounded cool and I should write it. I hope one day they'll read it.

Crash

Pete Mackley

Crash

Olympia Publishers
London

www.olympiapublishers.com
OLYMPIA PAPERBACK EDITION

A CIP catalogue record for this title is available from the British Library.

ISBN: 978-1-78830-656-0

This is a work of fiction.
Names, characters, places and incidents originate from the writer's imagination. Any resemblance to actual persons, living or dead, is purely coincidental.

First Published in 2020

Olympia Publishers
Tallis House
2 Tallis Street
London
EC4Y 0AB
Printed in Great Britain

Acknowledgements

I'd like to thank Steph for her patience and support in reading the original text, her constructive suggestions and for removing a lot of repetitive text. Overall, I'd just like to thank her.

To all the workers in the drug and alcohol services in Cornwall and Devon who I was lucky enough to work with: you are an incredible group of individuals who save lives as a result of what you do; it was a privilege to work with you. I learnt so much about people and life and although the characters in this book are entirely fictitious, I've borrowed a few real life incidents and then embellished them; I hope you don't mind, for one in particular I'd like to thank Xanthe, not just for that, also for being an inspiration and a friend.

I'd like to thank AA and NA for the amazing and tireless work that they do to support people with drug and alcohol misuse problems. They are like the fourth emergency service and don't get anywhere near the credit they deserve. I'm not in recovery, so I can say how they great they are; if you are having problems with drugs or alcohol, go to your local NA or AA meeting, get a sponsor and work the steps.

Kyle

He didn’t think rehab was the answer.

He’d been wrong about that investment and he didn’t have any money coming in. And yes, heroin was expensive, but it was good, and it took him to a happy place; there weren’t many of those left in his life now. His flat was shit, Westfront was shit, and this winter was particularly shit. Kyle didn’t normally get this reflective, but how had he got to this place?

Simon had appeared open and honest, if not even a bit gullible and successful; his business was due to expand into the South-west, and his recce down to Westfront attracted Kyle’s attention. A glass of red in the garden of the Pirate always gave time to sit and look at the people, to see if he could get anything or just have some fun at someone’s expense. He hadn’t seen Simon before and he looked like he was careless, with his words and his money. He was showing off, wanting people to know he was there and that he was wealthy.

Easy come, easy go. But what now?

Kyle had been seeing Jane at SWDP; this was the local drug and alcohol agency and they had an office in Westfront just off the back of a car park in town. It wasn’t great to look at, but it was full of caring people who looked like they had lives and maybe some knowledge and experiences to pass on. Kyle had been going to SWDP for a few months; he wasn't really sure why at first, but now he liked spending time with Jane. She was intelligent and caring, she listened well and seemed to want something different for him than the life he was living. He didn't know what that looked like and he didn't really get rehab or why he needed it. Heroin wasn't really a problem, especially now he got clean needles and the stuff he used was good; Sergei always made sure of that. The money was a problem, though. That bastard Simon had disappeared and £50K was hard to replace, benefits asked too many questions and he was running out of cash. The idea of not having heroin was almost as bad as the idea of working; maybe rehab was the answer. His sister Mary would sort the flat out, she'd put it in her name and that would take care of his capital. Mary was pretty easy to manipulate; she liked the attention and the control.

Kyle sat for a while looking thoughtful as though what he was about to say was really meaningful, he leant forward and spoke softly and meaningfully. He asked, "How can I go to rehab?"

Jane didn't show any emotion. She just said, "It's not that easy, Kyle, there's a lot to do before we can even think about rehab."

Kyle didn't like it when he didn't get his way. Jane was just supposed to start the rehab process, not start introducing barriers; he'd done the hard work by saying he wanted to go — why wasn't she just doing it? Kyle didn't think he should have to argue for rehab but maybe he had to play the game a bit.

"Come on, Jane, I've come off before, it's not great, but I can cope with the rattle; it's the lack of heroin afterwards that just doesn't seem worth it. There's just nothing to look forward to, if there's no drugs. Maybe rehab can give me that?"

Jane had been trying to sell rehab to Kyle now for about four weeks. It passed an hour or so a week. Kyle was almost looking forward to the time. He was reducing the heroin to the point that Sergei was pissed. Kyle knew he'd been a pretty good customer for the last three years. Unlike Jane, Sergei didn't care about Kyle, or apparently anyone. He seemed to care about expensive shoes and leather jackets and skinny girls with low IQs and no taste in men. He also cared about how much money Kyle spent with him, as though he was a column in his budgeting forecast spreadsheet and wasn't hitting the right numbers; his column didn't add up to a Belstaff leather jacket. Last year it probably did buy Sergei a very nice Belstaff jacket, some John Lobb boots and a whole load of accessories for his poncey wardrobe, but this year it didn't look like he'd be able to get much from Topshop, from what he'd made from Kyle. In fact, the last time Kyle saw Sergei his jacket was looking a bit tatty and probably could've done with being replaced. From what Kyle could tell the Topshop range was pretty good this year and some of their jackets looked OK from the other side of the road. Kyle thought maybe he'd suggest that Sergei take a look; he's always so amenable to fashion advice.

Jane started talking about detox. Kyle really didn't like the idea of someone controlling his reducing, and coming off was something he needed to control. Kyle tried to look like he was a bit worried or anxious, he'd practiced anxious before, as it worked with his sister Mary — she always wanted to do more to help if he could look and sound anxious. Through his anxious look Kyle said,

"If you could get me into rehab, I'd be clean for two weeks before. What a stupid thing to say, do you know how long two weeks is in Westfront with no drugs and not much money and feeling shit, whilst living in a shit flat and did I say in Westfront?" Kyle couldn't even take himself to the Pirate after he had fallen out with the landlord, who blamed him for Simon. He couldn't really afford the pub, and a glass of red always made him want some heroin — they just went together so well; being honest, though, most things made Kyle want some heroin — it just goes well with everything. And if he went anywhere, he'd likely bump into Sergei and his worn-out jacket and Kyle didn't need the grief.

Jane had arranged for Kyle to go the St's Place rehab for some sort of assessment. She was going to take him, as it was situated just outside the arse end of nowhere and she didn't think he'd find it. She didn't bloody trust Kyle to go; that was more like it. Kyle was ready to go now, though, he'd had enough, enough of living this bloody pointless life, no money, no drugs, no friends and just his dim bloody sister pointing out just what was wrong with his life and how he could do so much bloody better. It's a difficult argument really, because if he could do so much better, why hadn't he? She seemed to think that heroin was the answer to that. The only good thing about this meant that Mary didn't need any convincing to help with the flat. The flat was now in Mary's name, and Kyle was just a tenant struggling to pay the rent to a money-grabbing private landlady. Jane could probably help with that when Kyle was fixed and ready to leave rehab; he'd probably need lots of help.

So, assessment day arrived, Jane was going to pick Kyle up at 10:00 and drive to St's Place, leave Kyle there for one and a half hours whilst they did whatever they were going to do to Kyle and then take Kyle home. Apparently, they had a space. Jane had sorted out the money to pay for three months rehab; all Kyle had to do was pass the rehab's test. He wasn't really sure what was being tested, so he'd planned to just feel like shit and say he wanted to change. Jane was early, cheerful and loud. It was only 09:00 and Kyle hadn't had enough coffee or cigarettes or time or peace and quiet. He wasn't ready for loud and cheerful.

"Do you want coffee, Jane?" Kyle didn't imagine that she did; if she was this hyper without it, what would she be like pumped full of caffeine?

"No thanks, Kyle, I'll just wait till you're ready. I want to make sure we get to St's Place on time. It takes about 20 – 30 minutes to get there and I'd like to be early, first impressions and all that."

"I've not got to do impressions, have I? That's really unfair to include that in an assessment. I can only really do Brian Clough and he's been dead for ages — people might not recognise him."

"No impressions, just a figure of speech, come on, drink your coffee, let's get going."

Kyle couldn't go until he'd listened to Train, Drops of Jupiter, it was his soundtrack; it would be like it hadn't happened if he hadn't listened to Train. He pushed the start button on the CD and sat down to finish his coffee. He'd stopped listening to Jane now; Train were on. Five minutes later they were out the door walking to Jane's car, which was parked just by the gates to the park.

Kelly

Kelly woke up and looked around the room and wondered, what a shit place, whose place was this and who were these people? She got up from the stinking bed, unwrapping herself from whoever was still sleeping next to her. She got dressed as quickly and quietly as possible and stepped over two bodies intertwined on the floor, barely covered by a blanket. She got to the front door and closed it gently behind her. Never again, no more sex for drugs, no more drinking to oblivion, no more out of control, no more of this shit life. It had been like this for over ten years now, in fact it had been like this since she left that care home at 15. So that was 13 years and nothing to show for it except sadness and despair. She knew there was more, and she started thinking about that as she walked down the stairs away from that flat full of people, she hoped she'd never see again. The stairs opened out onto Boatyard Lane, just by the Happy Mermaid. How had she got from the Clipper to the Happy Mermaid? The same as always; promises for drinks, promises for drugs, too many drinks, too many drugs, too many promises and too many people. No more, now it was going to be different, no more promises, no more surprises, no more bloody loser people ruling her life. Right, sounds good, but just how exactly was Kelly going to pull this off? Rehab, that's how. Everything that she'd heard about rehab was not happening in her life now and everything in her life now was what she didn't want. Rehab should be perfect then; when could she start?

Kelly thought that now was as good as any time to start. She got the bus from Skittern to Westfront, walked into SWDP, and asked for Summer. Summer had spoken a lot about rehab, and Kelly hadn't really cared before but today she did, and where was Summer? Summer wasn't in today — she'd be back tomorrow; did Kelly want to come back? Not really, but she would. What would she do today, though? Westfront was shit with no money, sometimes it was OK to browse around the charity shops and maybe nick a top or two but not today. Today was the start of a new life, doing things right, no drugs, no crime, no fun, no shit. So, what could she do? Kelly went back to her room; it was in a shared house, her own front door, but shared bathroom and kitchen. She thought about tidying up the kitchen, she always hated what a mess it was, but she knew if she tidied it today it would just be a mess again tomorrow; nobody else bothered. Kelly seemed to crack first every time in the who's going to clean up game and no matter how much noise she made, no one ever took the passive aggressive hints and helped. Kelly just went to her room and picked up her book *The House of the Spirits* and started reading from the beginning again. Kelly loved this book; it had been a sort of gift from Summer, well a loan really, but without expecting to get it back. Kelly thought that was a thing with books, not with music but maybe with books. She might give it back one day but for now she'd start reading it again.

Kelly woke up hungry and angry. Why wasn't her life better? Her book was on the floor next to a discarded needle and she didn't have any food in the flat, just coffee and a cigarette. Sometimes there was a chance of breakfast at Breadline but for now she'd just listen to Amy Winehouse and drink coffee. Back to Black, everything seemed possible listening to Amy. Everything apart from breakfast, no food today. She headed down to SWDP to meet Summer, she wanted to be nice to her because she meant well and wanted to help but she just didn't feel nice today. She felt hungry, she felt sore, she felt sad, she felt angry and all those feelings seemed to roll into one gigantic not feeling anything like nice feeling. Maybe Summer would offer to take her out for breakfast; trouble was it was nearer lunchtime and she'd worry about food later. Now it was about finding that new life that other people seemed to be living, that other that she wanted that maybe Summer could get for her.

Kelly asked if Summer was in and yes, she was, and she was available. Kelly sat and waited in the hallway. Summer came down to meet Kelly, she looked bright and warm and seemed to just make Kelly believe that just maybe it was possible. Summer said,

"Let's go to the park and talk."

Then she just wandered off outside without waiting or looking for Kelly. Kelly tried to catch up, but Summer just kept walking; maybe today there was no talking until the park. Kelly quite liked the park, but it normally felt like it was just for normal people until dark and then it felt more like the place to go. Summer was nearly there, and she walked through the gates and headed for the café. She turned to Kelly and said,

"Do you want an ice cream?"

Kelly didn't have to think much about that.

"Yea, I'd love one, thanks."

Summer ordered ice creams and then handed Kelly a cone with a flake and then walked towards a quiet bench and sat down. Summer did that thing where she started talking whilst looking ahead. Lots of workers did that, Kelly thought; they must teach it on some course for communicating with difficult people.

"It's good to see you, Kelly, but you look quite poorly, what is it you want?"

Kelly thought for a moment and although what she really wanted was breakfast and then a pint of cider, she thought that maybe Summer meant something else, so Kelly answered, "I think I want to change, I've had enough, Summer, people treating me badly, the drugs, the sex, never having any money, never really caring, telling myself it's fun when it so isn't fun and I can't remember the last time I enjoyed myself and I want to meet someone decent and have a baby and a house and a family and be happy and think that something matters and look forward to something and I'm bloody starving and I want breakfast."

Kelly hadn't meant to say all that; it just sort of fell out — her filter definitely wasn't working today.

"Wow," said Summer. "Let's do something about that," and got up and walked back to the café, "Shall we get breakfast?"

Breakfast was great and more eating than talking, which was what Kelly needed. The coffee was when the talking started.

"How often are you using, Kelly?" Straight into the talking, thought Kelly, no small talk, no how was breakfast or this coffee's good isn't it. No, just straight to drug using. OK, if that's how it is then, Kelly started to answer.

"Every day, too much really, I can't afford it, I end up owing people and then doing stuff to pay them off." Summer had that knowing, supportive, caring look on her face, much better than that looking forward face she had earlier,

"Do you want to stop, Kelly?" Kelly tried not to look pissed off, she knew her filter wasn't working too well, so she tried to answer slowly; it didn't work — the words just fell out again.

"I so do, I just don't know how, I don't know anyone who has and I'm surrounded by a whole world of using, and every day is packed full of using and sadness, and they all look and feel the same and I don't want another year of that or another anything really, I just want it to be different."

Summer didn't judge, or her face didn't, she just leant forward a bit and gently said, "So, what about detox and rehab, it's a chance to get clean and then learn how to stay clean, with support afterwards and a real chance."

Kelly had heard about rehab, and her reply wasn't great.

"Amy Winehouse went to rehab, she even sung about it and she's dead."

Summer knew that a lot of people Kelly's age were deeply affected by Amy Winehouse's death and although all publicity about drug treatment was good, celebrities dying was hard work.

"Yes, I know, Kelly, but lots of people who complete rehab, aren't dead and they're living great lives. The NA is full of amazing stories of recovery and a lot of them started at detox and rehab."

Kelly didn't know much about NA or AA. She thought it was about God or something. Kelly didn't want to be negative but didn't know anything positive about NA. "I'm not sure about NA — isn't that all about God, and God hasn't been very much about me, has he? Look at me, Summer, do I look like God cares?"

Summer had heard it all before and wished that NA could get involved in marketing and publicity, but she knew it was all about one addict helping another and she knew that it worked. Summer kindly said,

"I don't think it works like that, Kelly, I think it starts with you and what you're going to do. So why don't we start making a plan? NA can be a part of it, detox can be a part of it and so can rehab, and we can even start to look after rehab as well. Firstly, let's talk about methadone and getting you off heroin, then you can start using your money to buy healthy food and start to live a little bit better."

Kelly didn't want to make a plan, she wanted to go to rehab; doing a plan sounded like a school project for stupid people. She wasn't stupid, and she didn't need to do any planning. She could just go and start changing. But Kelly knew that Summer would have to do some work and she supposed that would mean so would she.

"OK, Summer, what's first then?"

Summer seemed to talk for hours. Kelly had stopped listening. It might have been about her, but it was all too hard to hear. Looking back on this time Kelly couldn't remember how she'd even started on methadone and reduced to the agreed amount so that she was stable enough to go to detox; the last three months had just disappeared. Summer had been a great help, but Kelly couldn't remember when or how, not the details anyway. Today was the start, though, the day she was going to go to detox.

Summer had organised four weeks at CS Detox and then twelve weeks at St's Place rehab and had promised to sort out a flat at the end of it. It really did sound like what she'd wanted for years, so why wasn't Kelly excited or even a little bit up for the whole thing? Kelly really didn't know, but she'd packed her stuff and was heading out the door to meet Summer at the SWDP office in town. She didn't have much stuff, just a rucksack and holdall, some music, some clothes and a book. Most of the stuff she carried couldn't fit in a bag, it was deep in her soul, but most of the time it wasn't that deep and it overflowed from her mouth and her body in ways that sickened her, not today though.

Today was a start, and Summer was going to drive her to detox and then leave her there. Summer had said she could play her Amy CD on the way. Summer was waiting outside for Kelly, just finishing off a roll up, and Kelly thought how nice she was; if it had been different, Summer was the sort of friend that Kelly would've liked. Kelly gave Summer a card and just stood awkwardly thinking she shouldn't have bothered. Summer smiled and opened it; it was a picture of Westfront sea front and inside Kelly had just written Thank You. Summer stopped and fought off the urge to cry just a little.

"Kelly, that's lovely, thank you so much. Come on, let's get going, have you got Amy with you?" Kelly liked that; Summer had remembered, that's what she liked about her: she listened, she cared, the little things as well as the big things. Kelly rummaged in her bag and pulled out the Amy CD,

"Come on then, Summer, let's get going."

Rehab — Assessment

The drive to St's Place didn't take that long and Jane swung her car into the gravel car park, There were a few run down outbuildings but the main building looked quite imposing; it was an old Mill House that looked as if it was a long time since it had been used for any industrial work. The grounds were basic but well kept, with grass, shrubs and a few trees. The property looked as if it had been extended a few times, but it all fitted together quite nicely. Kyle and Jane got out of the car and walked in through the five-bar gate to one of the outbuildings that had been converted to an office. An old, half-panelled wooden and glass door opened, and a middle-aged woman stood there with her hand outstretched.

"Hi, I'm Cathy. I'm one of the team at St's Place and I'll be doing your assessment, you must be Kyle?"

They shook hands and Jane walked into the office and said hello to a couple more staff. They introduced themselves to Kyle but he didn't hear; he was trying to work out Cathy and what it was she wanted from this assessment.

Cathy started walking to the main building. "Come on, Kyle, we'll go and get this assessment started, would you like a tea or coffee?"

Kyle thought about a drink. "Yes, that would be great."

They stopped to talk to a couple of inmates, residents, service users or whatever they were called at St's Place, and one of them went off to make Kyle a drink. Kyle took the coffee that was offered by the vaguely familiar looking bloke who was holding it out. Kyle didn't hear the name or if he did, he couldn't remember it. Kyle was normally more in control than this, but it was all unfamiliar and there was a lot going on. Cathy looked back and said, "Bring your coffee, Kyle, you can spend some time meeting our residents before you go today."

Cathy walked into the main building and into an office off the hallway and Kyle followed into a sparsely furnished but bright office: a desk, a couple of chairs and a coffee table; there was one of those motivational pictures on the wall, something about change. Kyle always thought these were naff but today he was OK with the idea of change; at least on the surface, he didn't mind the idea of looking like change.

They sat down and Kyle put his coffee cup on the table. Cathy opened up a clipboard and started talking about St's Place. The potted history of the rehab took about five minutes. Kyle didn't really know the history and he didn't really care — he just wanted to get on with it.

"Does this sound like the sort of place you'd like to come and make a start to your recovery, Kyle?"

Kyle didn't have to think too hard about that but wanted to appear thoughtful. "Yes, it sounds just great, and it's a lot nicer looking in real life than on the website."

Cathy smiled. "Yes, we need to make a few improvements in that department. OK, Kyle, can you tell me a bit about yourself now, specifically some history about your using and what brought you here?"

Kyle didn't want to give too much away but wanted to say enough to get in. "I've been using heroin for years now, not at the moment. I got off at home, I said I'd be clean for two weeks before I came here and I have been, I am clean. It started in my twenties, just a weekend thing, but pretty soon it became an everyday thing. I started using with a girlfriend, but the heroin lasted longer than she did, it's lasted longer than most things have. It's been most days for fifteen years. I never thought it was a problem, but it started being more important than other stuff, well more important than anything. I'd either make bad choices or no choices. Other people and things stopped being important, my sister still talks to me, she helps me out sometimes, but other than her it's just me now. I've not been working, I've given up my flat, I've lost whatever savings I had left, and I couldn't see a way out unless it all got very different. So here I am, looking for different."

Cathy had been listening and concentrating, watching Kyle's body language and listening to the words. She thought there was something not quite right or not quite true about Kyle and his story. This wasn't unusual; most people who came to rehab were manipulators and quite capable of embellishing a story or two to get what they wanted. Cathy believed that if people could experience a bit of time clean and some positive role modelling, a bit of care and attention, then maybe, just maybe change could happen. People had said of the staff at St's Place that the staff loved me until I was ready to love myself. Maybe some of that love would help Kyle to settle down, find himself and find his truth and get some recovery going in his life.

The assessment carried on for about an hour and a half, more of a conversation than anything else. Cathy was listening for commitment to change, a hint of desperation, the idea that Kyle had had enough of his life and his bad decisions and that he was ready to do whatever it took to make recovery happen. Cathy also wanted to know that Kyle wasn't a risk to staff or himself or other residents and that he'd fit into the community they had at St's Place. Cathy closed her clip board and said, "We're all done now, Kyle, I'll introduce you to one of the residents who can show you around and answer any questions you've got. I need to talk to my colleagues before we can offer you a place, but assuming I could offer you a place would you want to come?"

Kyle hadn't expected that, but he hadn't come here to say no. "Yes, definitely, Cathy."

Cathy nodded and said, "I'd like you to phone tomorrow at 11:30 and if everything's OK, we could be looking at you coming here this week. Is that OK?"

Kyle thought it was all a bit quick, but what difference did a few days make? He didn't have any plans, so this week was OK. "Yes, this week would be great, Cathy."

Cathy got up and put out her hand to shake Kyle's and smiled and looked him in the eye. Kyle shook her hand and held eye contact; it was easy for him — eye contact didn't mean anything to him. Cathy walked off into the main building and turned to make sure Kyle was following; they walked into a large dining room where people were sat doing what looked like schoolwork. A man about Kyle's age stood up and spoke to Cathy. Cathy said, "Thanks, Dan, I'd really appreciate that, and when you're finished just come over to the office."

Dan smiled at Kyle and asked, "Do you want to have a walk around the place, Kyle?"

Not really, thought Kyle, he'd had enough pretending for today. He just wanted to go home and get away from all these people. Dan seemed all right, though, so Kyle promised he'd play nice for a bit longer. "Yeah, that would be lovely. It's Dan, isn't it?"

Dan walked and talked as they went around The Mill. The décor was shabby, but the place did look homely even though up to twenty people lived here at any one stage; they had sixteen at the moment. The kitchen was well equipped and modern; Dan explained how everyone mucked in and cooked the meals and shared the food. Kyle thought it sounded like a hippy commune. Dan must have picked up on Kyle's thoughts as at that moment he said, "It's not like a hippy commune, though it sort of looks like one sometimes. We do all hug in the mornings after we've said the Serenity Prayer."

Kyle thought that with all probability it was going to be hard work at St's Place. Dan walked through the lounge and into another hallway and up some stairs to the first floor. It looked like there were five or six rooms. Dan explained that there were seven bedrooms on this floor and six on the next; there were another seven bedrooms in an adjoining house. Dan opened a door and stepped into his room. "Come in, Kyle, we're not supposed to have people in our rooms, but it will be OK today as I'm giving you the tour."

The room was homely, with good quality chunky pine furniture and adjoining shower and toilet. The large window had views of the grounds to the rear of the building and across the valley towards Weytown. You could just see the top of the old Mill wheel which Dan explained was where they stood when they completed and got a framed photo stood in front of the wheel. There was no TV in the room; just a bed, wardrobe, drawers and chair. But it looked comfy and warm and Dan had personalised it a bit with a couple of pictures of what looked like family. Kyle didn't ask. Dan headed off back to the dining area and introduced Kyle to a handful of other residents; some looked quite poorly but most of them looked well and seemed to smile readily and all of them tried to make Kyle feel welcome. Dan seemed to know not to make it last too long and was aware of how uncomfortable hellos can be if they go on too long. Dan started to walk off.

"Come on, Kyle, Cathy will be waiting, and we've all got work to be getting on with, haven't we?" Everyone looked up, nodded and said a collective goodbye. Kyle decided that maybe rehab was the answer and this lot looked OK.

Cathy opened the office door and asked Kyle to come in and sit down. Jane was sat at the table with another person. Cathy smiled. "Kyle, this is my colleague Phoebe, the rest of the team aren't in today, but I hope you'll get to meet them soon. Jane and I have had a lovely catch up — we go back a long way. We've done all we can today, Kyle, the next part of the process is that you need to go home and think about if this is what you want and then phone me tomorrow at 11:30. We're done now unless you've got any questions." Kyle reckoned that he probably should have some, but he hadn't planned this part, so he just shook his head and Jane got up to leave, she hugged Cathy and Phoebe and walked off towards the car. So that was the assessment, thought Kyle, it went OK and he thought if they offered him a place tomorrow, he'd say yes. Jane opened the car and got in. Kyle got in and hoped that Jane was just going to drive, but apparently, she wasn't.

"How did that go then, Kyle?"

Kyle shrugged, he knew Jane couldn't see that as she was driving, so he decided to answer but with minimum words. "OK, I think, I've got to phone Cathy tomorrow."

Kyle stared out of the window at the countryside as Jane drove back towards Westfront; the outskirts of Weytown were pretty and the narrow roads and high hedges made it seem as if they were miles from civilisation; there was just countryside everywhere. Kyle was thinking about how time at St's Place would be, and he thought it would be quiet and very different from life in Westfront. In this part of the world twenty-five miles was a very long way. Jane had tried to open up a conversation a couple of times, but Kyle had appeared to be in deep thought and not at all receptive. Pretty soon Jane was driving into Westfront.

"Do you want me to drop you at your place, Kyle?"

Kyle wasn't sure. Did he want to go into town and risk everything that going into town involved, or did he want to carry on laying low for a few more days?

"Drop me at my place please, Jane."

Jane pulled up outside and just before Kyle got out Jane said, "Well done for today, Kyle, you came across very well and I hope you get to go to St's Place. I think it will really help you get your life in order. I'll phone tomorrow and find out what the answer is."

Kyle turned to Jane and smiled slightly. "Thanks for all you've done, I think it was good today, I'll phone you tomorrow after I've spoken to Cathy at St's Place. I think they want me to go there." With that Kyle got out of the car and walked up to his front door, he turned and smiled and waved to Jane, who was already driving away. Kyle went inside his flat. It didn't really feel like home, it had always been just a place to eat, sleep and use. He hadn't ever brought a girl back here; he always wanted to keep this place private. When he looked around now it didn't mean a thing to him, no memories of anything really, just a place where he'd spent five years and the best part of £200,000 and all he had to show for that was the chance to go to rehab. Not much to be proud of there. It looked quite different when he was the top salesman in the South-west at ClearUConservatories and Simon's conservatory roofing company had looked like it was going to rescue his year, not send it plummeting to the top of his all-time list of shit years. Worse than the year he got caught manipulating the figures in his favour at ClearU and had to leave without commission on seven big jobs. In fact, the last five years had all been pretty shit. It really was time for a change, and maybe staying clean from heroin was worth doing, well at least for a while anyway. Kyle turned the radio on, not really to listen, just noise. Radio 2 wasn't great in the afternoons but the music was generally from times when life was lighter and when there had been less going on. Kyle wasn't nostalgic, he didn't care about the past, he just wanted some excitement, some sort of buzz, like a big sale, an important deal, that first use of heroin, getting away with something, or the idea that his life was just a little bit out of control so he needed to think and work hard at staying ahead, not just drifting along like it had been.

There was a knock on the door. Kyle didn't like visitors, but he answered anyway.

"Sergei, what are you doing here?" Kyle was surprised to see Sergei. Sergei looked pleased with himself. Maybe it was a new jacket, Kyle wasn't sure, and he wasn't going to ask; he didn't want Sergei knowing what he was doing and he didn't want to let him in his flat. “I thought you might need some stuff, Kyle; I not see you in a while and I worry.”

Kyle thought quickly. “You need to stay away, Sergei, the doctor thinks I might have TB, it’s very contagious. I’ve got to go in and have treatment. I’ll be gone a while.”

Kyle was pretty pleased with that answer, and Sergei obviously understood as he started walking off before he said, “Get well, bye.”

Kyle went back in and sat down and tried to quieten his mind. It didn’t really work; he was hungry and Sergei turning up had made him think about heroin. Maybe if he had some food, he could get through the day and not do any damage to his chance of rehab. Kyle dug out the chicken pasta he’d frozen and put it in the microwave; he wasn’t a good cook and thankfully he was worse at portion control. The last time he’d cooked he’d made enough pasta for today as well. There wasn’t much else in the freezer, but the fridge might keep him going for a couple more days. Propaganda, Duel was playing on the radio; that always made the day a bit better, no reason — it was just one of those songs. Not a great song like Drops of Jupiter but a feel-good song. Kyle wanted to get some stuff from town before rehab and thought he’d venture out to charity shops after he’d eaten his pasta. It wasn’t much really, just a couple of books, Kyle thought; a couple of spiritual journey books would look good to everyone else. Kyle was pretty sure that charity shops would have that sort of thing. Kyle’s chicken pasta wasn’t great when it was fresh, and reheating it didn’t improve it; it was barely functional but probably contained enough nutrients to get him through the day, if he hadn’t given himself food poisoning. Kyle thought he could ask Mary down for a couple of days. She could make him some meals, keep him company and then drop him at rehab, she'd then have the keys to the flat so she could clean it up and rent it out. That worked for Kyle; he'd ring her when he got back from town.

Town was busy, it was the start of the holiday season and the weather wasn't great, so families of tourists were milling annoyingly in and out of all the shops, just looking to waste time, get in the way and maybe buy some naff souvenir to remind them of their lovely holiday to Westfront. Kyle thought he could manage a couple of charity shops before it would all be too much. The local animal hospital was first, and Kyle thought they must have been to the charity shop recruitment consultants because the staff were stereotypically exactly what he'd expected them to be, no high pressure sales here, just slightly passive aggressive gestures and a couple of middle-aged women trying to look busy but not doing anything. Kyle went to the book section and surprisingly found *The Alchemist* by Paulo Coelho; this was perfect. But nothing else in the animal charity shop. He paid for the book £1.00, a pretty sound investment, and cut the woman short who was trying to tell him how much she'd enjoyed the book and how it had changed her life. Kyle said "thanks" and left. British Heart Foundation was next, and Kyle was now expectant that he'd find another book; he only wanted three and he might even read one of them. The Heart Foundation had been to the same consultants as the animal charity, Kyle thought, charity shop staff were from a mould, but he headed through the busy shop to the books; all these people and no service, he cynically thought. Not too many books but they did have a self-help section and there was book number two, *Way of The Peaceful Warrior*, by Dan Millman. He thought he'd ride his luck and head onto shop number three. Barnado's was next and although the staff were the same, the book selection was pretty poor, so Kyle committed to one last try. Cancer Research was so busy; there were people pushing to get in and out. Kyle didn't mind a bit of a shove; social conventions like politeness never bothered him. He pushed his way through, surprised with the ease that people moved out the way. Once in the shop Kyle noticed two more staff from the charity shop mould and he headed to the books. They didn't have many, but they did have *The Shack* by William P Young, which would've been a shoe-in for his spiritual collection if it hadn't been for that film with Sam Worthington; not that Kyle had seen the film, but the reviews had been enough to put him off and it made the book too popularist for his list. Then there it was: he saw exactly what he needed, *The Teachings of Don Juan* by Carlos Castaneda. £3.00 in total and three books to look like he was on a journey; he didn't need anything else now, just to click his heels until he could go to St's Place.

He wandered back to his flat, pleased with his afternoon trip to town. He was running the conversation he wanted with Mary in his mind and had stopped noticing the bustle of Westfront at teatime. He got back to his flat and started getting things ready to pack; he didn't have much, just some walking boots, shoes, a couple of pairs of jeans, some tee shirts and a few fleeces and three quality books and some music, Drops of Jupiter the album by Train, and The Coral and Yoshimi Battles the Pink Robots by The Flaming Lips, but that was only there for the rhyme, fight them and vitamins, which just made Kyle laugh every time he heard it. He could take Our Town by Deacon Blue which had Twist and Shout but also a great cover of I'll never fall in love again which had Kyle's favourite lyrical rhyme, of catch pneumonia and never phone you. Just brilliant. With that Kyle phoned Mary. She was easier than she should've been, she so wanted to help and think that she was doing her bit to support him. She was going to take some compassionate leave and her husband was going to look after the kids whilst she planned to be in Westfront for about 3:00 tomorrow afternoon. Kyle thought that was great as it gave them time to go to Morrisons and get some food, so she'd be able to rustle up a few meals, before he was off to rehab.

Kyle slept pretty well last night. It was rare for him to sleep past 9:00 but today it was halfway through Pop Master when he turned the radio on. The kettle drowned out the sound of the questions and when he sat down with toast and jam and his coffee it was Three in Ten by some band he'd never heard of, but he wasn't really listening. He had a phone call in under an hour and although he didn't like to worry about things, this call had his attention. Cathy answered the phone and Kyle said "hello". Cathy sounded very nice on the phone; there was softness to her voice that was very calming, Kyle thought she'd do well in a call centre or some customer complaints line.

"Hello Kyle, have you had chance to think about coming to rehab?"

Kyle definitely had. He was packed and ready to go, getting ready to let go of his old life. "Yes, I have, Cathy, and I'm ready to come. It's definitely what I want."

Cathy smiled. That was what she wanted to hear; now was the time to find out how ready. "We've got a place now, Kyle, so will you be able to get here tomorrow about 11:30?"

Quicker than he'd planned, but no problem. "Tomorrow it is then." Again, Cathy was happy with that, no hurdles introduced that didn't need to be, she didn't like emotional fencing at this stage.

"Great, we'll see you tomorrow at 11:30. Have you got a lift?"

"I should have, my sister's coming down, but she's not here until this afternoon."

Cathy thought about that and then offered, "Well, if anything goes wrong, just ring us by 10:30 and we'll come and get you, see you tomorrow." And then she was gone, it was done, rehab was actually happening, his new life was starting, but more importantly, his old life was finishing.

Detox

The drive to detox went really quickly, Amy on quite loud and Kelly feeling strangely excited, was this really the start of something new in her life? Summer could feel the energy and just let it run, no need to say much, in fact nothing to say; Summer had worked hard to get funding for Kelly for Detox & Rehab; all she had to do now was make sure Kelly stayed and didn't do anything to get kicked out. That might sound simple, but Summer knew she had a lot of work still to do supporting the staff at detox to get Kelly through and then the same again once Kelly got to rehab, plus a lot of supporting Kelly. Amy was just finishing as they pulled into the car park at detox. It was a modern sort of bland building that sat in the countryside just outside Weytown and although quite large and surrounded by a fair amount of land there were no people walking around; everyone was obviously inside today. They walked into reception where a couple of friendly women made Kelly feel very welcome. There was lots of paperwork and Kelly hated filling in forms. It made her feel stupid; she could read OK but it took her a long time to understand some sentences and she didn't want to ask in case she looked stupid. So, she just nodded and signed stuff. Summer stayed and did everything but hold her hand. Kelly felt supported and safe even though this was way outside her comfort zone; still she hadn't properly gone in yet. The paperwork wasn't finished but enough was complete to move into the main building and have some lunch. Kelly and Summer were led through the main corridor into a sort of clinical type place with a big lounge, pool table and table football and a few people sat around chatting and just passing time. Kelly knew that look and it wasn't what she wanted anymore; she wanted to make the most of her time, do something with it, make something happen, stop just accepting that shit is just what happens.

Different, from today it was different, is different. The office was just off the lounge with a big glass front, so nothing was going to be missed. A smiley hippy woman came out and said, "Hi Kelly, I'm Lena, I'm your key worker, we'll get to know each other over the next few days, but welcome to detox, let's go get some lunch."

Kelly followed Lena through the lounge and felt eyes following her every step. She was obviously the new girl, and everyone was deciding what she was like and making guesses as to what her story was. Kelly didn't mind this, she sort of expected it — she'd been the new girl before and probably would be again; they could think what they wanted, but if they wanted to know they'd have to ask. The dining room was off the lounge and looked great, all wood beams across the ceiling and wood panelled walls; bright coloured chairs around pine tables gave it a sort of café feel and already about ten people were eating lunch. The food looked okay; Kelly thought this place seems just fine. They queued for lunch behind three others at a help-yourself hot food counter. The people in front all turned and said hi, Kelly mumbled a hi back and Lena started telling Kelly who everyone was: some were residents some work staff, nurses, keyworkers, support workers, doctor and managers. It was a lot to take in and Kelly must've glazed over as Lena said, "You don't have to remember all the names, Kelly, I just thought it would help if you knew a little bit, just ask if you don't know, remember you're the new girl."

Kelly was pretty hungry; she could hear her stomach growling and the chilli looked and smelt great. She didn't want to appear greedy, but it did seem like a long time since she had eaten anything. She looked around to see how much food other people had put on their plates and tried to match the amount. Lena had about half as much.

"Don't worry about me, Kelly, I'm dieting, you get plenty of food in you."

Kelly felt she had enough, and smiled and said, "If I'm still hungry, maybe I'll go back for seconds." The idea of seconds always made Kelly happy; her first foster parents sometimes let her have seconds. That was a lovely memory, shame about their son — she didn't like to think about that.

Lena and Kelly sat down at a table with three other people and they just chatted about nothing really for the duration of lunch, casual chat but intense looks. Kelly just ate her chilli, she wanted to go back for seconds but too many people were watching. They didn't have to wash up, just rinse everything and then put it in a great big dishwasher. Lena suggested Kelly go outside and have a smoke and then they'd get together to sort out the rest of the admission process, get her into her room and meet the senior nurse.

Kelly sat outside on a well-made sturdy wooden bench, in a smoking area on the edge of a courtyard. It was shaded from the sun, but bright and airy and she started to roll a fag. Before she'd finished a thirty-something year-old man was sat next to her; he looked like he'd lived a full and varied live and most of it had involved drugs and trouble. He put out a hand to shake Kelly's and said, "Hi, I'm Andy, welcome to detox. What you in for?"

Kelly didn't know how much information to give and what the rules of engagement were. She'd hoped to have had a bit more time before she was in a position like this, one on one and not sure of the rules.

"Hi Andy, my name's Kelly." Kelly put her head down and rerolled her fag, she started paying attention to the roll up enjoying the ritual, ignoring Andy. Andy just started talking, he wasn't even looking at Kelly — he was just talking and talking. Kelly finished her roll up and got up and started walking around; she thought if she looked anxious and nervy, Andy might shut up and leave her alone. Andy wasn't skilled in reading body language or in taking notice of social cues and got up and started pacing with Kelly.

"I like to walk when I'm a bit anxious," he offered Kelly.

Kelly went inside and started looking for Lena. She knocked on the office door and Lena came out. The next few hours were a blur of meeting people, sorting out medication, signing forms and moving her stuff into her room. A support worker had searched her stuff as she unpacked and made sure she hadn't brought anything in. The rules had been explained, pretty simple: no drugs or alcohol, take your own meds, no sex and no violence. There were loads more rules, but those were the ones that mattered.

Kelly's room was nice. It had a barred window out onto the garden and the furniture was modern and functional — bed, wardrobe, easy chair, coffee table and a cabinet with an en suite shower room. Kelly thought she could manage four weeks here and if detoxing was going to feel bad, at least she had a comfy room to feel bad in. She put her clothes away and sat and just enjoyed the quiet; this was her space and it felt nice. She had some time before dinner and getting her meds, so thought it best to be seen by everyone else. She didn't want people to think she was avoiding them, she didn't want people to think anything really, but that was too much to hope for. She knew she was the new attraction, and everyone wanted to find out what and who she was. She went into the lounge area and sat down with her book. Pretty soon all the seats around her were full and the conversation was about her. Kelly gave the minimum information, from Westfront, coming off heroin, going to rehab, been in care all her formative years, been sort of flitting around various places for drugs and money and she'd had enough. People listened and related similar stories. There were nine people chatting and another five were around the detox but not here now. They all got up and walked through to the dining hall for dinner, more chat and more anxiety. Kelly just wanted everyone to leave her alone, stop asking her questions and just let her get on with getting better. There was a film to watch after she'd had her meds and she managed to fake enough interest in the film for everyone to leave her alone. Bedtime came eventually and Kelly almost ran to her room, to the quiet and calm that her own space offered and to a night's sleep in detox. She picked up her book and put Amy on to get rid of the day, she didn't really want to get rid of all of the day, she wanted to be here and the staff seemed nice and the food was good — it was just the people she wanted to get rid of, not all of the people but definitely a few of them. Amy helped and rehab started. Kelly just loved this album and instantly she was taken away from the intrusive people she wanted to not be there and off to a place somewhere near happy. She started reading *The House of the Spirits* again. Maybe one day she'd actually read it all but for today it was chapter one again.

The first couple of days were a bit of blur for Kelly. People were manageable as long as she didn't give the men one to one opportunities. The girls seemed safe. All the staff seemed fine; she felt they were on her side. A couple of the groups had been a bit intense but she could just glaze over for a bit; that seemed to work for her. Lena said they were going to have a proper session in a couple of days, so until then she'd carry on keeping a low profile, doing no harm and keeping away from trouble. The problem was trouble was looking for Kelly. That evening Andy managed to catch Kelly unaccompanied in the smoking shelter and started acting like her long-lost friend, sitting too close, and then his hands started to touch as he spoke. Kelly moved away but Andy followed and then, when he was talking, he put his hand on her jeans and started to move up. Kelly thought, but not for long enough because suddenly her cigarette was pushing into the back of Andy's hand and she was walking back inside the building. Andy never mentioned that moment again and neither did Kelly, but they both knew it wasn't the end and that Andy would cause Kelly plenty of problems throughout their time at detox. Andy didn't care, he knew people like Kelly and usually they just gave up and eventually let him do what he wanted; Kelly just thought she was different. Andy quite liked a bit of sport; there wasn't much fun to be had in detox, so he'd take it where he could.

Kelly went to her room, Amy was waiting ready to make it OK, "Love is a losing game" not really appropriate but better than listening to Andy and his bloody touching annoying hands. Kelly thought how to deal with him, she knew he was going to try again, she'd normally just give up in the past and take the hit, let him have what he wanted and maybe just get some drugs or rob him when he crashed, but not now; now she was doing things differently, not letting drugs rule her life and not living at the whim of people like Andy. This was going to be hard work. Getting off methadone was going to be a breeze, getting away from her past lifestyle was where the work was needed. Kelly thought she needed a friend, she'd not had a friend since leaving care, she got close to someone once but that was a long time ago and Max had been special, he understood, he'd been through everything as well. He didn't judge and he didn't want anything, he'd just been there when she needed someone. But Kelly hadn't seen Max for ten years; they just drifted apart, drink and drugs and squats and a lot of water under a lot of bridges. Kelly had nice memories and thoughts whilst Amy sang her soulful heart out trying to make everything better. Thinking of Max was good but Kelly needed a real friend now, someone to keep her safe, someone to keep Andy away from her and someone to just be with, to talk and hopefully laugh and think about better times, maybe even share some hopes and dreams. Yes, Kelly thought, she definitely needed a friend.

The weekend came quickly and there was a buzz around the place, no groups and a relaxed schedule, but for once in her life Kelly had a plan and although the choice was limited, she was going to find a friend, and they were going to be lovely, and supportive and as good as Max. Better than Max actually, because Max wasn't there now and Kelly needed a friend now, not a memory of what a friend was, but an actual friend. Saturday morning after breakfast Kelly made herself available, she let her guard down and sat in the lounge, and just chatted to people. Kelly kept it gentle and tried not to look desperate or have too much of an agenda. She knew everyone would pick up on that and she didn't want to look like she was being manipulative. The rest of her cohabitants were just not good friend material, in fact they were a lot like her, and Kelly wanted friends like Summer, who were clever, non-judgemental, warm, happy and full of life. That wasn't the type of people that she was looking at here in rehab, but she had a plan and maybe she'd have to compromise on just a couple of things. The first thing she needed to be was patient. Kelly hadn't been patient much in the past, she hadn't had much practice. Instant gratification was more her style. If she wanted something, she wanted it now and generally she wasn't bothered about the cost, but recovery felt different. Kelly did care about the cost today, she wanted what she wanted but not at any price. If she carried on like this, she'd have to develop discernment or at least stop making really shit choices. Sam seemed wary of Kelly, probably not just Kelly — she was probably wary of everyone. It looked to Kelly like Sam was about her age, but it was hard to tell. Kelly asked about Sam's family and just tried to be interested. Sam smiled and said, "Let's go and have a smoke, we can chat outside."

Kelly and Sam stood up and walked out to the garden, a couple of the blokes got up as well but both Sam and Kelly looked at them and they sat down straight away.

As they sat down on the grass away from the building the sunshine warmed their skin and there was a warm breeze which reminded Kelly of a trip to the beach when she was younger, a day she liked to think about and remember what it feels like to not have any worries. She actually always had worries when she was in care, but she didn't take them with her that day at the beach. She rolled a smoke and handed it to Sam as she rolled herself another. Sam and Kelly talked and laughed for three hours, no-one bothered them, it hadn't been deep but it had been friendly, they listened and paid attention when each other spoke and they allowed each other to tell their tales, talk about their experiences and share their fears about detox. They also had a common goal to keep Andy at bay and not let him near them.

This was perfect for Kelly, a friend and ally all in the same person. They both grew up in Cornwall but in different parts and different care homes, they'd both had their share of trauma and both had too many drugs and too much alcohol. It normally weighed heavily on them but today there was a lightness about them both. Maybe Sam had been looking as hard for Kelly as Kelly had been for Sam.

They got up and went in for lunch, they didn't talk about this; it just happened — they seemed to be in sync with each other. Kelly wanted to eat outside but they weren't allowed, so she sat at an empty table in the corner, with her back to the wall. Sam did the same, that way they could growl and stare at people who wanted to join them. Nobody came over for most of lunch and then Andy joined them, sitting down as he said, "You don't mind do you, ladies?"

They obviously did mind, but Andy didn't care; he fancied a bit of sport as so far, his Saturday had been pretty dull. Sam and Kelly got up together and both said, "Enjoy your lunch, Andy." That felt good for Kelly. She finally felt she was starting to put a boundary in place and better still, holding it. They talked about this in group and Kelly hadn't really got it; her boundaries had been pretty non-existent before; now things were different, and her behaviour was starting to change. Sam and Kelly walked outside and were chatting like old school friends as they went and sat on a bench round the side of the building.

Sam asked, "Do you think he'll ever give up?"

Kelly thought about it and although she wasn't sure, she had an air of confidence about her answer. "If we keep holding the boundary like that, he won't change but he'll give up on us."

Kelly and Sam had both found the friend they wanted and their journey through detox was faster and easier because of it. The thing was they were both due to go to different rehabs, Kelly The Old Mill and Sam The Manor in South Devon. They couldn't change as funding was from different counties and tomorrow was Sam's completion at detox and move to The Manor. Kelly had been assessed by Cathy from The Old Mill and was due there the following week.

They all sat around the lounge in a big circle and Lena started talking about how well Sam had done and how her journey of recovery was just starting. The things she said were lovely and Kelly felt happy for her friend, but she also felt an overwhelming feeling of sadness at the loss of her company. Everybody spoke about Sam and how lovely she was and how well she'd done. All the residents including Andy and then the staff, then it was Kelly's turn. Kelly started to say how lovely it was, but then the tears just started and she sobbed and sobbed, from deep inside; she couldn't control it and she just turned and hugged her friend and cried all over her shoulder. She'd kind of said goodbye earlier and they swapped numbers and promised to keep in touch, but now all Kelly could do was sob great gulping tears.

The next week dragged but Kelly made it through. No Sam, that made it harder but well-held boundaries carried on working and soon Kelly found herself sat in a circle with Lena saying how far she'd come. Kelly didn't really hear any more; the whole circle spoke, they were saying nice things and Kelly didn't really have a place to file those, so they just drifted around the room not making contact with Kelly. Afterwards Kelly said her goodbyes, gave a few hugs, no one asked for her number and she wouldn't have given it. Kelly went to her room and grabbed her bags, Amy and *The House of Spirits* and walked out through reception to the waiting taxi ready to take her to The Old Mill.

Rehab

Mary turned up as promised just after Kyle had phoned Jane. Mary was delighted that Kyle was going to rehab tomorrow, she'd waited ten years for Kyle to take some responsibility in his life. She was fed up of him leaning on her whenever he needed anything. She told herself that today was "one last time" unless he actually did change in rehab. Kyle pretended to be pleased to see Mary; at least he'd have some decent food now that she'd turned up to cook something. "Hi sis, are you staying long? 'Cos I haven't got any food in. We'll need to go and get some."

Mary knew that meant she'd have to get some as Kyle never had any money for sensible things like paying bills or buying food.

"Just as long as it takes to get you into rehab. Then I'm straight back to my family, so let's get some food, then I'll cook us a nice dinner."

Kyle thought that went OK, but he wasn't bothered if it hadn't, he was going to get a tasty meal and Mary was going to rent his flat out, which he would've struggled to be arsed to do. Mary drove to Morrisons and they chatted on the way about her kids; well, you could have called it chatted, but Mary talked, and Kyle listened enough to interject with the right word to give the impression he was listening.

Kyle didn't really want anything else from Mary. She'd committed to do what he needed, so he didn't see the point in trying anymore.

"What shall we have for dinner then, Mary?"

Mary got the message, dinner and breakfast, then she'd be driving home back to normal people who appreciated her and loved her for what she did. Kyle always just took and sometimes Mary found that exhausting; now she was just plain pissed off with the whole thing. Today it was finite and finished after breakfast tomorrow. She parked the car and walked into the shop, Kyle following. Mary got two lamb steaks and some broccoli and new potatoes and some sausages, eggs, bread and butter. Some coffee and just for kicks she picked up some non-alcoholic lager, she also picked some bathroom supplies and a couple of tee shirts, some pants and socks and thought that just about added up to her sisterly commitment.

"Let's get going, Kyle. I need to start rustling up some dinner." Mary paid. Kyle didn't try to pay, or offer to pay, or mind.

They sat down to a delicious dinner and talked about rehab and maybe even after rehab and what a life without drugs might look like. Kyle was happy to play the game and even said maybe he could be Uncle Kyle when he settled down and got back into work. Between them they painted a picture of a life worth living, one that Mary would be proud to have Kyle live and maybe one that Kyle could be bothered with pretending to live. It was a pleasant evening; the time passed quickly and easily, nothing contentious, just nice pretending.

Breakfast was the same, and then it was time to get Kyle off to rehab, no surprise that Kyle couldn't leave before he'd heard Drops of Jupiter; he was always weird about that. All Kyle's stuff comfortably fitted into a medium-sized holdall. Kyle realised that really was all he had. They left the flat and Mary locked up. She'd get the management company involved later; now she just wanted to make sure that Kyle was at St's Place and that they were responsible for him for a few months. Mary turned into the car park at 11:20. She'd always been good at being on time, being responsible, not getting into trouble and lots of other things that Kyle wasn't good at. As they got out of the car Cathy walked towards them and offered her outstretched hand to Kyle.

"Welcome to St's Place, Kyle. I hope you find all the things you've been looking for."

Kyle introduced Cathy to Mary, Cathy hugged Mary and said gently into her ear, "Don't worry, we've got him now."

Mary walked back to her car and couldn't hold back her tears as they gently flowed; maybe for the first time in 15 years she didn't have to worry about her brother. She allowed herself the luxury of believing that and drove home smiling and feeling warm inside. It wasn't long before she was back with family and for once not worrying about Kyle.

Kyle followed Cathy into the office. Phoebe and Chris were inside and welcomed him warmly, no hugs yet, just smiles and handshakes. The hugs would probably start later. Cathy explained about induction, bag search and paperwork, but nothing would happen now until after lunch, Cathy walked over to the main building and came back with Dan. Dan smiled and said he was going to be Kyle's mentor for the first couple of weeks and Dan laughed, saying his first job was to make lunch for Kyle, better than Kyle had expected — another sap to cook for him. They walked over to the kitchen and Dan made a plate of sandwiches with salad and crisps on the side and then they went into the dining room where about ten others were sat eating various things on toast or in sandwiches. The chat was friendly and polite and from what Kyle could tell quite respectful. Dan introduced everyone and said that another five would be down later, so in all there were seventeen residents. Dan said that number was awkward as the minibus only had sixteen seats, which meant that the logistics of going anywhere got a bit more complicated. The mix of people was twelve men and five women and fairly equal between drug and alcohol misuse problems. The age group spanned from mid-twenties to sixty, but most people looked older than they were. A snapshot of addiction taken around the table at St's Place would show that addiction isn't good for you; this wasn't a roomful of healthy people. Throughout dinner Dan was very attentive and kept putting names to faces so Kyle could follow conversations and not feel left out. The conversation moved quickly, and more people sat down, more smiles, more hellos. Kyle already had a sense of feeling OK at St's Place. One of the topics Kyle could understand was as there were now seventeen residents and a sixteen-seater minibus, it meant that someone was staying in tonight, instead of going to the AA or NA meeting. People seemed to volunteer willingly and allow other people to voice their reasons, requests were listened to and very quickly a consensus was reached. John, who appeared to be in some house leadership type role, said he'd let staff know after lunch.

The next few hours just flew by. Kyle completed paperwork and was duly inducted, his bag was searched, well sort of supervised as he unpacked in his room. His room was very similar to one he'd seen when Dan showed him round. Cathy led the process skilfully and assertively with the impression that she was being gentle and patient. Kyle noticed the procedural efficiency of St's Place and how he was being managed by Cathy and he appreciated what was being done.

Cathy explained the rules. They were simple: no alcohol, no drugs, no violence, no acts of aggression and no sexual relationships. There were a few other rules, but they were more about guidance and as such were much less black and white and were managed rather than enforced. Cathy left Kyle in his room with his stuff out on the bed and said, "Enjoy the rest of the day and enjoy the meeting tonight, stick with Dan — he'll look after you and I'll see you tomorrow morning after group."

Kyle sat down and thought about the day so far; he was actually in rehab and it didn't seem too bad. He was a little disappointed that no one had commented about book choices; he'd probably have to read them now so someone could see how spiritual he was, but not today; it was time for some music and then down for tea. Kyle started putting his clothes away, he thought he'd start off tidy, at least maybe he'd tidy up again after three or four weeks, he could listen to Train for the rest of the evening but he had to go and meet everyone and play at being the new guy.

The lounge was filling up as Kyle thought that schoolwork was finished, some people were watching TV, some reading books and quite a few were outside by the smoking hut. Kyle chose the smoking hut and noticed that Dan and John were both out there.

"Hi Dan and John, sorry I don't know everyone else yet."

The other three introduced themselves and the chat carried on. Dan explained it was ham, egg, chips and beans for tea and it was being made now by three of the residents; they took it in turns and one of John's jobs was to sort out a rota for meals and chores. Kyle cringed inside; he didn't like rotas, but he guessed that nobody liked them apart from accountants.

After dinner there was an hour to kill before they were off to an AA meeting in one of the local towns. Kyle was expected to go to five meetings a week and three of them were to be NA. The minibus went out six nights a week and everyone stayed in on Friday. Kyle could see that St's Place was a well-oiled machine; there wasn't much free time, what with groups, meetings, chores, meals and then schoolwork; it wasn't really schoolwork — it was Step work, but it was a lot of writing about using, consequences and feelings. Kyle knew he had all this ahead of him but for now it was the food of kings followed by an AA meeting.

This wasn't Kyle's first AA meeting and he knew it wouldn't be his last; he struggled with the idea of powerlessness and didn't like the concept of a higher power. He knew he'd have to get over this to successfully get through his time at St's Place, which people seemed to refer to as The Mill. At the meeting tonight he just listened and watched. Apart from the crowd from The Mill there were about twenty-five people in varying degrees of desperation. Most of them looking for something they were unlikely to find but some of them were happy to share their journey with people seeking the same. It was sad and yet tinged with hope, and that made it quite compelling to observe. Kyle thought to himself he could have some fun with this group of people and just maybe there was something in it for him, not recovery, but control and power. Kyle liked those better; they were real things he could feel and experience, things that were worth working towards, not momentary fleeting feelings but strong guttural feelings that lasted.

It wasn't long before they were back at The Mill smoking and talking about the powerful share that one of the residents had done. Gemma talked about how alcohol misuse had led to her losing her kids to Social Services and how now she was working at getting herself right so she could hopefully get her kids back in her life. She was doing it one day at a time and that helped her get through the difficult days and to stay patient when she wasn't getting anywhere. Kyle used all his inner strength to not say blah, blah, blah, he'd heard it all before and most of the time nothing changed; he kind of wished Gemma well but didn't see much action yet, just words about how it wasn't fair.

Kyle slept well for his first night in rehab and after breakfast it was time for the morning group. Cathy, Phoebe and Chris walked in and sat down. By 09:00 the rest of the house were already seated, and Cathy started by saying good morning and welcoming Kyle to the house. It was confirmed that Dan was Kyle's mentor and Cathy said that she'd give Kyle some work to be getting on with after group which followed this morning meeting. There were a few house notices, the diary was read out, one of the residents recited out a reading, Kyle listened in case it was relevant but his mind drifted because he'd heard it before.

Phoebe leant over to Kyle and asked, "You don't mind hugging, do you?"

Dan had been right: they did hug each other like a hippy commune. They all stood up, held hands and recited the

Serenity Prayer, like in AA but then they went around the room hugging each other, somehow staying on the right side of appropriate, and everyone at least pretending to take it seriously. Kyle thought it wasn't a bad start to the day, just a bit weird.

There was time for a quick smoke before group and then everyone was back seated in the main room, Phoebe looked like she was leading, and Chris sat opposite her.

Phoebe said, "This is feelings group, Kyle, just listen and come in before the end, we've seventy-five minutes and everyone has to speak. Okay everyone, it's your group."

Gemma started by talking about how she felt relieved after sharing last night but talked herself round to frustrated because it was taking a long time. Her feelings were real but not very revealing. This was the theme around the room, no great depth to anything but enough to show some feeling and a slight amount of reflective commentary. Kyle felt he could manage that and talked about being anxious, not really knowing anyone or anything about life in rehab, but he was here and a little bit excited about that. He'd obviously revealed enough, and it moved on until everyone had spoken. When it was over, Phoebe got up and walked out the room closely followed by Chris, who hadn't said a word.

Everyone was outside smoking and chatting and Kyle felt nothing. He didn't know who was real, who was vulnerable and who was faking it. It was just a blur at the moment; he knew this feeling wouldn't last — he just had to wait; he couldn't observe and fake emotions at the same time — it took too much effort. Cathy came over and asked Kyle to come to the office when he'd finished his cigarette.

Kyle walked out of the office, with his first assignment; he had to write a life story. It was to be four pages of A4, and he would read it to the house in a group in three days' time. Kyle wasn't sure about this. He didn't want to reveal all but equally he didn't want to look like he was holding back, but in all honesty four pages was never going to be the whole story. He thought about the problems that drug use had caused, the losses, the friendships, the family traumas; he could easily manage four pages and hold some back if he needed a share that no one had heard before. Kyle spent the afternoon writing about how his family gave up on him, apart from Mary, but he knew she was close to tether end and he didn't have many chances left. He wrote about a childhood that wasn't difficult but one that left him bewildered at times. He hadn't understood or connected with the other children; they always seemed so needy; he didn't write that but he thought it, then and now, people seemed so needy, always looking for some form of confirmation and reassurance. Kyle never wanted or needed either. It was during his teenage years that he became distanced from his parents and he moved out as soon as possible, not wanting to abide by arbitrary rules any longer than necessary. The world of work wasn't great either, but Kyle had a flair for sales that the double-glazing industry was keen to both exploit and develop. As a teenager Kyle worked in a showroom and converted browsing couples into quality sales leads much better than any of his older colleagues. At eighteen Kyle progressed to showroom sales, followed quickly by external sales; he liked the buzz of selling, but it didn't last, and salespeople liked to say they worked and played hard. To Kyle that meant drugs, and he was offered lots and took lots, and whilst most of the sales team liked coke Kyle found heroin hit the spot: it calmed him, emptied him, almost centred him in a way he hadn't experienced before. Selling got him up, drugs brought him back and took away all the stuff in the middle. Kyle felt his life was starting to shape, selling conservatories was easy, taking heroin was lovely, he didn't need anything else, he'd taken the odd bit of coke when out with colleagues, as that was what they all did, but when he got home it was heroin that did the job.

He didn't want anything else, the occasional girl would come along, he liked them clever and sultry — he didn't mind what age and he wasn't too bothered about them or what they wanted. They just seemed to come and go; he couldn't remember the names of some of them and the faces seemed to meld when he thought about them. He couldn't really remember if any of them were important and he didn't miss any of them, nor want to see them again. He wrote about a couple of them and that they left him because of his drug use; this was true, but they would probably have left him anyway. He wrote about how it all went wrong with his family because he just couldn't be arsed to go and see them when Mum was ill, he couldn't be arsed when she was well, why would that change when she was ill? He kept in contact with Mary; she seemed to need it and it worked for him, he let her help out occasionally. It made her feel important and, he suspected, better than him. He didn't mind as long as it worked for him.

Kyle wrote about how he mismanaged his drug debt and thought he'd cleverly skim some money from sales at the conservatory company. He never thought they were that professional that they actually knew all the details of his sales and how his banking was always a couple of thousand out. He thought he could bluff it out when they first challenged him but they actually had all the figures spanning nearly two years. That was enough to put him in prison if they took it further. Kyle paid it back, left, paid off his drug debt and sat in his flat pissed off and down to less than £80K. He needed to make some money and he couldn't sell double glazing in the South-west because news travels; then along came Simon. Kyle was obviously stupid and desperate, that's a great combination for any con man and here we are today, skint and needing to change, ready to stop heroin's control over him and start thinking before acting. Understanding actions and consequences are more often than not linked; if you're not careful, it's really easy to get to a place that you don't want to be. Like Kyle, nearly homeless, skint and in rehab.

Kyle read it out to the other residents. Every time he said you, he was made to correct it to I. Apparently that personalised his story and made it contain real feelings. Kyle just felt it demonstrated pedantry of the highest order but he went along with the game, ending his story with "it's really easy to get to a place I don't want to be, homeless, skint and in rehab". Kyle tried to fake the odd emotion whilst reading it out, to make it look like it hurt and that he was sorry and that some things had a hint of guilt or remorse, but they didn't. He genuinely wasn't bothered. He'd told his story but it could have been a story he'd read in *Reader's Digest* for all he cared. The residents seemed to relate to certain parts and a couple of times people wiped their eyes but for Kyle it was mission accomplished, he was one of the gang and in a position to manipulate and cajole as and when he needed, or so he thought.

The next couple of weeks went by without much incident for Kyle. He attended AA and NA meetings, he shared at a couple, no one cared about the validity of what he shared, just the depth. People related and surprisingly wanted to hug him. Kyle noticed that at The Mill people were quick to relate, quick to cry and quicker to hug. It was a strange place full of strange people living strange lives. But here was the weird bit: Kyle felt at home, he didn't understand that piece of the jigsaw or any of the jigsaw, come to think of it; the more he faked it the more he liked it and the more it liked him.

John's completion ceremony was the next big event but before that happened Kelly arrived from detox. Kyle liked her. She didn't meet the criteria intellectually but visually she ticked the boxes, and he was prepared to compromise when there was a relatively small talent pool.

In the morning everyone sat around in a large circle with Phoebe and Cathy either side of John. Behind John on the sideboard was an amazing cake that a couple of the residents had made last night. Everything was celebrated by cake in recovery, no champers or popping corks or lines or clinking bottles, just cake. To be fair, it did look like a bloody good cake and it was made with love high up the ingredient list, because everyone loved John. He'd been like some sort of invisible glue that held everyone together, a beacon that everyone could see and aim towards. Phoebe spoke first about the unrecognisable addict that had arrived at The Mill twelve weeks ago, the challenges he brought with him and the difficulties he had until he let go. Phoebe really wanted to say "Let go and let God". She knew that sometimes that got the wrong reaction, she and John both knew that was what happened. After that recovery just happened, changes in behaviour and attitude just collapsed from John. Without any apparent effort he became a senior peer when he had no seniority, he took responsibility when nothing was expected from him and he became accountable for his life. He stood up and wanted to be counted for the first time in his life and as far as he could see his life was full of hope. Phoebe spoke with love and eloquence and authority; it was easy to believe that this man was more than the total of what could be seen, and he really would be missed. The whole house echoed this sentiment; each resident had a story of how John had been a friend, a shoulder to cry on, a font of wisdom or a mixture of the three rolled into one with half a dozen other virtues added for good measure. Then everybody ate cake. It was as good as it looked and if the secret ingredient was love, it should be sold in supermarkets so it could be added to all cakes and maybe other things too.

After cake everybody walked out to stand by the old Mill wheel. John was surrounded by the cohort that helped to shape him and a photo was taken for him to take away. Phoebe turned it around quickly and the photo was printed, signed and presented to John in an expensive looking frame. All the residents had bought and signed a card and book. The book was an AA text, and John was delighted with the warmth of the messages and the journey he'd been on. He said some words, thanking the staff for all they'd done, how they'd believed in him and most importantly for helping him find the person who must have come to rehab with him, but he'd never really met before. He cried and hugged everyone, saying thankyous and giving messages of encouragement and hope and promising to come back to the weekly aftercare sessions, also committing to meet up at AA and NA meetings in the area. A taxi arrived and whisked John away to a future of hope-filled recovery, everyone clapped, a few people whooped and cheered, nearly everyone cried. There was no cake left and no John. The Mill had a piece of its superstructure missing.

Kyle had a one to one with Cathy while Kelly was being inducted by Phoebe. The rest of the house went inside and licked their wounds. Kyle and Cathy sat in a small office cradling hot drinks and not really saying anything. Cathy was observing, taking everything in. Kyle was trying to give nothing away. Kyle talked about missing John, not really the physical being, more the idea of what John was. Cathy understood but wanted Kyle to talk about Kyle. Really, she just wanted to start him on his first Step Work assignment and get a feel for how he was settling into the house and to the AA fellowship. Kyle was pretty sure he could get away with faking his progress, but he had a feeling that Cathy suspected something and that she wanted more. He quite liked the dynamic, the sort of intellectual and emotional fencing, he never tired of these games and he had the feeling that neither would Cathy. She was a worthy adversary but not really the therapeutic relationship that The Mill tried to create. Cathy knew it wasn't happening yet for Kyle, but she thought if he pretended hard enough, he might just get it before the end.

The next two weeks flew by. Kyle worked on his Step assignments and Kelly just loved everything about every aspect of The Mill; she loved the groups, the residents, the AA and NA meetings and the feeling of being at home. Even though it was only temporary she felt at home, like a part of a great big family, sharing meals, trips out, being there for each other, being allowed to be sad and being allowed to be happy; this was what she'd needed in her life for a long time. She kind of liked Kyle but thought he was a bit distant at times, she guessed he had a lot going on; everyone seemed to have a lot going on, but he was easy on the eye.

The next morning's house meeting, unusually, was attended by all the staff; this normally meant something was going on. When everyone was seated Cathy spoke. "We've had some news from The Manor in Plymouth and want to pass it on to you. Some of you knew Sam in detox. Unfortunately, Sam left rehab early and she relapsed and died. There's going to be a memorial service and if anyone wants to go, we can make arrangements."

By now Kelly was wailing; strange noises kept coming from somewhere deep inside her. Sam was occupying a space somewhere inside Kelly's heart somewhere that she hadn't let anybody into for years and now she was dead, taken by bloody drugs; she was so lovely, so full of life, so dead, so wrong. Kelly couldn't get up from the floor. Kyle was holding her hand, not saying anything, just being there and holding. Kelly needed that, she needed more but not now. She needed Sam, she loved Sam, she hadn't loved for a long time and this was why, because loving bloody hurt, not like lonely or abuse hurt, love hurt completely — her whole body was consumed with pain, physically, emotionally, mentally it was like every atom was crying and screaming, and Kelly couldn't imagine it would ever stop. Nobody else had really known Sam; a couple of people had met her in detox, but it was only Kelly that loved her, that knew her, that understood her, that missed her, that needed her, but Kyle was still holding her hand, feeling strong and supportive, being strong and supportive.

Cathy suggested everybody take 15 minutes to have a smoke and then come back in for the morning meeting. Kelly just couldn't get up. Phoebe came and helped Kelly up.

"Kelly, take as long as you need, the day can happen when and if you're ready. For now, I think someone's made you some tea, stay around the communal areas so we know you're OK but don't worry about anything else, your priority is you, take care."

Kelly leant on Kyle. She didn't mean to, but he was solid and strong, and she wasn't; she needed solid now she was crumbling. They went and sat in the lounge, Kyle still holding her hand. Kelly needed Amy; Kyle wanted her to listen to Train. After what seemed like forever Kelly went to her room, she needed Amy, she couldn't be with anyone, she wanted Sam, she didn't even have a photo. How could she love someone so much and not have anything to hold? She needed Amy.

Kelly put Amy on and hoped she'd work her magic, she was falling apart and she needed to put herself back together, she needed rehab and recovery and she needed to be strong. Kyle felt strong; maybe she needed Kyle, not now, now it was up to Amy. The day at The Mill was quiet and subdued. Everyone wanted to keep checking on Kelly, but they wanted to let her have some space and time. The general view was that tonight she needed to go to the meeting; when shit happened, meetings helped. Everyone knew that, but no one really knew why; recovery was mystical sometimes, but so was life. Kelly went to the meeting, she didn't want to, but she didn't want to stay at The Mill whilst everyone else went, she needed people. The meeting was a blur, the day had been a blur but when they got back Kyle made her a drink and rolled her a smoke and asked her if she was OK. Kelly felt safe; she talked, and she didn't cry. She talked about Sam and friendship and how close she was and how recovery was different. Kyle listened and nodded and seemed to understand. He told Kelly about his younger brother and how on his brother's 21st birthday, Kyle took him to try some drugs; Nathan was the wild one, he never had any fear and overflowed with confidence. Kyle took him to a friend for some heroin. Nathan didn't want some, he wanted loads, well, all of it really. Nathan crashed and Kyle went out to get some beers. After that Kyle wasn't sure of the details, but there was a police raid and as Nathan was crashed his so-called friends stashed the drugs on Nathan. When Nathan was arrested, he had enough Class As to supply a small village and he took the rap for everyone else, keeping Kyle completely out of the picture. Nathan never went to prison; he hanged himself before he got there; he was 21. Kelly was heartbroken for the second time that day. She barely knew Kyle, but he'd been through so much like she had, she just felt like being with him made her feel better. Kyle glowed inside; it was exactly the thing that Kelly needed to hear, if only it were true. Kyle never really had a brother at all, but Kelly didn't need to know that. Kyle would tell the story about his brother a few more times but never as powerfully as to Kelly.

People completed at The Mill and new people arrived. The place ebbed and flowed with energy and recovery. Some got it and lived the values of The Mill, some fought against it, but mostly people seemed to be overpowered by the force of recovery that flowed through The Mill. The staff were tremendous, determined, dedicated and caring, full of warmth, forgiveness, compassion and patience. Occasionally this overflowed into frustration and the odd cross word was spoken, but mostly they were saints. Groups were used to move people and to learn, then reinforce new behaviours. It was a conveyor belt of change. Lots of the groups were emotional train wrecks but sometimes they were comedic insights into the minds of addicts. Residents went through a rollercoaster of emotions and were supported by their peers with love and understanding in a way that most of them had never experienced before. People thrived at The Mill, mostly after about the first four weeks. The first month was the hardest; however, towards the end people wanted to stay, to cling on to the idea that recovery was like this, life at The Mill was real, but it wasn't real life. For most it was home and the best home they'd ever had, and it was family, the sort of family they wanted, not the sort of family most of them had.

John came back each week for aftercare, not because he needed it but because he missed the place, the staff and the way of life. No matter how well he was doing he hadn't felt as well or as needed as he felt at The Mill; The Mill made him better, made him want to be better. Being better didn't make that much difference outside The Mill; life just drifted on. He went to meetings, he didn't drink, and he met friends for coffee, but he didn't have the purpose and drive that he had at The Mill, so that's why he came back each week. To touch the magic and try and take it away with him. People still saw him as the inspiration they thought he was; he just didn't feel it, he was empty and sad, and recovery was hard.

Kyle was nearing the end of his time at The Mill. Cathy and Jane had been working together to get Kyle a flat in Westfront. They didn't know he owned one and that his sister had rented it out. It was nearly sorted; the council had a fund to supply furniture and there were charities that supplied white goods and paid agency fees. In two weeks' time, Kyle would move into a furnished flat and a life where he didn't have to work for six months because the social paid. It was what he'd wanted when he started this journey, now he wasn't so sure. Kyle hadn't planned on meeting someone, but Kelly wasn't something you planned on; she just happened. She filled a space and then there was more of her. She'd completely affected Kyle; he actually wanted to be with her, he didn't want to live with her, he didn't really want to share that much, but he wanted Kelly in his life. He even thought about keeping up with AA and NA because he knew Kelly liked it. This was new for Kyle — actually thinking about other people, not because he wanted to control or manipulate them but because he liked them and wanted to be in line with them, alongside them, not them but definitely Kelly.

Everyone sat in a circle with Cathy and Phoebe either side of Kyle. Behind him was a cake. Kelly had made it; it was completely full of love; there was chocolate and cream and strawberries, but mostly love. They didn't buy the love from the supermarket; Kelly just gave it, she had loads, losing Sam hadn't closed her off, loving Sam had opened her up. Cathy spoke with kindness and hope; she hadn't been deeply moved by working with Kyle, more gently challenged really; Kyle had been interesting, not inspiring, and Cathy wasn't convinced he had enough recovery in the bank to make it, but it was up to him — he knew what to do and now he had to do it. His peers were the same; no one had been deeply touched or moved by Kyle — he'd been OK; he always knew what to say and when to say it, but sometimes it seemed a little contrived as though it were an act. No one said that, but it was implied. There was no congruence, no integrity, just a well-presented front. Not for Kelly though; she loved Kyle, she wasn't going to miss him because she'd see him at meetings and at the weekend, she was going to spend a whole day with him.

They all ate cake. The cake was amazing; everyone complimented Kelly on how amazing it was, everyone spoke with mouths full of cake. Nobody minded — it was a celebration; things were celebrated best with cake. And this was good cake. Kelly had thought there would be some left over for Kyle to take with him, but every last crumb was gone. Kelly thought that maybe she could make him his own cake and take it at the weekend. That was a nice thought and felt warm and cosy inside. Kelly liked doing things for people, especially when it was appreciated. Kyle wasn't that bothered about cake; he preferred savoury food, meat mainly, but things at The Mill weren't celebrated with meat. The preferred accompaniment to an event was cake, so Kyle played along, and he knew Kelly had made an effort and that was what mattered.

They all gathered around The Mill wheel and Cathy took a photo of Kyle and the residents all huddled together looking proud and just a little uncertain. Kyle was given a card and an NA textbook, signed with lovely messages of hope and gratitude. Kyle said a few words, he thanked the staff for helping him see a future he believed in and thanked all the residents for supporting him and caring for him. He promised to come back to aftercare and he looked forward to seeing them at meetings down west. He couldn't wait for the taxi to come. He hugged everyone and some people actually cried. Kelly waited until last. She'd never really said a proper goodbye to anyone she cared about. They hugged and Kelly cried; she couldn't speak, she knew what she wanted to say but there were no words. Kyle hugged her tightly and said,

"I'll see you at the weekend, we've got a whole day together."

With that Kyle was gone, staff and residents whooping and cheering and clapping as the taxi disappeared up the drive. Kyle was dropped off outside his new flat. It was just over a butcher's shop in the main part of Westfront, far enough away from where he lived before for him to have a new start. He thanked the driver; it was pre-paid, so he just grabbed his stuff and went inside. It was small but clean and bright and free. He plugged in his CD player in the lounge and got his Train CD out of his bag, he put Train on and sat and just let time drift away.

After Rehab

Kyle hadn't planned his life post rehab; he'd worked hard to get into rehab and to get this flat but here he was now, in his new place, not really knowing what to do and why to do it. Even more complicated now was that he had another person to think about. He liked Kelly; she'd been a surprise, she was just so there, more than other people he'd known. He wanted more from Kelly, but he wanted to do it slowly, patiently and gently with respect, not like he normally was — it was normally just about him and his needs. The conquest was the most important thing but Kelly: well, he wanted more. The rest of his life was less certain. Jane had sorted out a volunteering job for him at a local market garden, nothing too taxing and certainly no shop work stood looking busy whilst doing nothing. Kyle couldn't have coped with that, but a bit of gardening sounded OK. He thought he'd ring Mary and maybe offer to go and see them next week, see the kids and her husband and let them see how well he was. Maybe he'd ask for a car to help him get to all the meetings. They always had a bit of money stashed away since Dad died so they could afford to help him out; he'd just have to ask a bit delicately.

Maybe he could offer to pay them back from the rental income from his flat. Mary had done a pretty good job securing

£500 a month after management costs and the tenant seemed pretty permanent. Kyle was planning on going to aftercare each week at least until Kelly completed rehab, but probably for a while longer to keep Jane happy in case he could get anything else from her. He was going to keep going to NA meetings as well, mostly for Kelly as she liked them. Kyle found them just a bit annoying, all those shares that he didn't care about and that desperation to save people, just let them fail; it wasn't like they were ever going to do anything with their lives. Today, though, he needed some things to get through the next few days. He didn't have any food and he didn't actually have much in the way of pots and pans or crockery. Kyle wasn't sure if he could manage Argos, he found the idea of buying from a catalogue a bit strange, he knew they'd have everything he needed but he couldn't bring himself to go there. Sainsbury's was going to be more expensive, but it was a better-quality shopping experience and better-quality stuff. Maybe if he phoned Mary first, he could get her to help with all the stuff he needed? He'd tell her about Kelly and wanting to cook her dinner. Mary was bound to be impressed by that.

Sainsbury's had everything Kyle needed: plates, cups, cutlery, pots, pans, all good quality and all beautifully coordinated. Mary had agreed to chip in £50.00, plus she'd sent him a list of food to buy so he could make a special meal for Kelly and not starve for the rest of the week. Looking after himself was harder than he remembered. He never bothered with it that much when he was using; a box of cereal was good enough for three meals a day and the occasional burger whilst he was out. Actually, buying food that needed cooking was very different; the whole thing seemed to take up so much time. Not too much time tonight, though, because he had liver and bacon and mash to heat up in the microwave and a bottle of coke to wash it down with, no alcohol and no drugs, times definitely a-changing.

Kyle checked out Netflix on his laptop but thought he ought to go to a meeting instead. There was NA in Westfront tonight and The Mill crowd would be there, so he could let everyone see how committed to recovery he was. Liver and bacon accompanied by the Coral; it was hard to listen to Dreaming of You without wanting to dance, but today Kyle would settle for eating instead. Whilst he was eating Kyle was thinking how useful a car would be. Getting to a meeting on the bus was going to be an event. Maybe he would get a lift back from someone; he definitely needed to pitch harder to Mary about his car. Public transport wasn't Kyle's favourite, but he got to the meeting in plenty of time for under £2.00. He didn't buy a return as he was sure he'd get a lift back. There were a few people milling outside the room where the meeting was. Kyle recognised some of the group who were smoking and chatting. Most looked well and were full of confidence, recovery and good humour. John was there, not looking well and certainly not looking full of recovery. It looked like he'd relapsed, and he'd gone downhill a long way; this wasn't the John Kyle had known at The Mill. John looked ruined and beaten by guilt, shame and what Kyle later heard was a three-day binge of drugs and alcohol ending with a night in the cells. Today he was facing up to the music and was being supported by his sponsor; but on the condition that John shared his story tonight. Kyle could see how uncomfortable John looked and spared him the embarrassment of talking to him. The minibus from The Mill arrived and Kelly jumped from the bus and ran up to Kyle. It was like being greeted by a puppy. Kyle really liked it; Kelly was special and made him feel good. He was really glad he'd chosen the meeting over Netflix, he told Kelly all about his day and how he couldn't wait until the weekend when they would spend the day together; then it was time to go in for the meeting. Everyone went in and the meeting started. There was some hope and some recovery and when John spoke of his last few days, everyone could feel the agony he was going through, the loss of his recovery, his sense of failure, his heart-breaking disappointment, his feeling of helplessness and his utter sense of worthlessness. People supported him and thanked him for sharing and a few other people spoke. John was beaten and the people from The Mill were devastated; if John could relapse, then what could happen to them? The mood on the bus back was sombre. Nobody really talked about John, nobody knew what to say. Kelly wanted to talk about Kyle but didn't think it appropriate, and she cared about appropriate now. It was an early night for everyone at The Mill tonight. Kyle got a lift from one of the men who was driving past Kyle's road who dropped him off but didn't stop. Kyle was grateful for the lift and for not having to do too much small talk. He quite liked that with Kelly, but he didn't feel judged by Kelly; that was a new feeling for Kyle.

The weekend came around quickly and Kyle had arranged to meet Kelly at the train station at 10:30. They would have the day together and then meet up with the crowd from The Mill at the meeting in the evening and Kelly would go back with them. Kyle had prepared lasagne and a salad, and he'd bought some posh garlic bread. As he prepared the food last night, he thought how well a bottle of Rioja would go with dinner. Instead he'd bought a bottle of red grape non-alcoholic bubbly. If only he could've got some non-heroin heroin for dessert. Dinner just needed to go in the oven and the rest of the day was free. Kyle walked to the station and waited outside watching the people. He was hungry but he was going to have breakfast at a café with Kelly. The train arrived on time and Kelly was the first out of the station, bouncing along like Tigger. Kyle walked towards her and she jumped into his arms. Kyle was lost in enthusiasm, hugs, hair and kisses. Kelly couldn't help herself; it just fell out — she said, "I love you". Kyle thought about Patrick Swayze in *Ghost* and thought "ditto" might do; he hadn't expected it and he didn't know how to respond. Kelly just seemed to be able to throw him slightly. He liked that, but he wasn't sure about love or ditto.

"Kelly, you are so amazing. Let me buy us some breakfast so I can sit and look at you."

Kelly thought she'd got away with it, she didn't want to put Kyle off. He was the best she'd known in years and she felt so special when she was with him, amazing seemed pretty cool and she really wanted breakfast.

They walked hand in hand. She'd never walked hand in hand with a boyfriend; this was just perfect. The sun was shining. Westfront was busy with tourists but Kelly couldn't see anything apart from her perfect world; the only people living in it were her and Kyle. They sat outside the Bay Tree café in the sunshine and just started talking. Throughout the conversation the waitress took their order for coffees and full English breakfasts with everything. Kyle listened a lot, he knew that worked and every now and then he reached across the table and grabbed Kelly's hand and just looked in her eyes; he didn't always time it right, but Kelly didn't mind. She felt like she had a proper boyfriend, someone who cared about her, even respected her, someone who didn't just see her as payment for drugs and someone who just wanted to be with her. This was so close to what Kelly thought normal was that she never wanted it to end.

Kyle was enjoying breakfast. Kelly was a good-looking girl and she was fun to be around. He never knew quite what she would say or do; she had a childlike innocence about her, and he liked that. After breakfast they held hands as they walked along the front and looked at the boats in the harbour, at the sun glinting on the sea and shining through the whites and silvers of the rigging of the sailing boats. Not enough wind for a busy day sailing; most of the boats were just bouncing alongside a buoy. Kyle liked it better unspoilt by people. It wasn't too busy. Neither of them wanting to do anything apart from enjoy time together, they meandered along the front and then cut up a side street heading towards the gardens. Kelly could feel an ice cream coming. Kyle had treated them to breakfast and Kelly had enough money to buy them both an ice cream and still have enough left for the collection tin at the meeting. The park was beautiful; the sunshine made everything look better. Neither Kyle nor Kelly knew the names of trees or plants or birds but the sights and sounds of the park were magnificent, both of them in a heightened state of sensory awareness being substance free, both having learnt about paying attention and being in the moment, that sense of mindfulness where it was impossible to miss the wonder of the park and of nature.

They sat on the grass and let nature entertain them. The moment lasted, but soon they were talking and touching, arms and hands as part of the conversation, just light touches, but sensuous and caring, almost loving, as if words weren't enough. Kelly wanted a great big ice cream cone with two chocolate flakes and sauce and sprinkly things. She dragged Kyle up and pulled him towards the café so they could have ice creams.

"Come on, Kyle, it's my treat." The ice creams were enormous and lovely. It had already been the best day ever for Kelly as they wandered back to Kyle's flat, holding hands and licking ice creams.

The streets were still busy with tourists walking slowly and milling around. Kids carrying buckets and spades and parents looking pink from sunburn. They walked up the stairs above the butcher's and into Kyle's flat.

"This is just great, Kyle; you'll be so happy here, there's everything you need."

They kissed, a welcome to my flat sort of kiss, not a let's have sex kiss, almost a friends' kiss, but Kelly liked it; she was having the time of her life. Kyle put on the Coral as background as he started faffing around in the kitchen.

"Can I help with dinner?"

Kyle smiled. "No, I did most of it last night. I've just got to put it in the oven."

Kyle set the table, with his new Sainsbury's dinner set that matched the pasta dish in the oven, a chic water jug and glasses and the bottle of safe fizz and glasses. Since the care home no one had cooked Kelly dinner, bought her breakfast, walked along the front holding hands and then sat in the park and spent the whole day being her boyfriend.

The flat wasn't big but it was big enough for a jive when the Coral started singing Dreaming of You. Kyle could dance enough to lead Kelly into moving the right way at the right time and Kelly just loved it, jiving, what else could possibly happen? Dinner was wonderful, dancing was amazing, Kelly didn't want the day to end, but they had to go to the meeting, and she had to go back to The Mill. The meeting was dull, no John, no relapses, no interesting shares, just recovery happening, slowly filtering through the group. The Mill wanted it, needed it and there seemed to be plenty of it at the meeting. But it was time to go back now and Kelly didn't want to go. Kyle didn't want to walk home and be on his own; normally that was his favourite, but today had been great. They kissed goodnight. It was a very different kiss, thank you for the day, goodnight, stay safe and see you soon; there was even some I love you in that kiss.

The last two weeks at The Mill went quickly for Kelly. Phoebe and Summer had worked together really well to secure a flat for Kelly in Westfront. They both felt she needed the best start in her life and the most support they could give her. She was embracing everything about recovery, but she was so open and vulnerable that made her a real worry. It was also Kelly's turn to be house leader. Kelly was really scared about being leader of anything, but the staff at The Mill liked everyone to have a chance to experience leadership and positive mentoring and it only happened if people were ready.

Everyone knew that Kelly was ready. Kelly had embraced all The Mill had to offer. Recovery was like the gateway to a new life. All that was wrong in Kelly's life had gone and it had been replaced with a sense of joyfulness, an appreciation of wonder and hope. This was new for Kelly: hope, the word said so much about how far Kelly had come in just a few weeks. Kelly liked to stop and think about the future, her own flat, her boyfriend, a job, a future, a family — yes, Kelly kept thinking about having a baby. She hadn't said anything to Kyle; letting

"I love you" slip out was very different to "let's have a baby". That could wait, the dreaming couldn't.

Being house lead was quite daunting. People asked Kelly for help, for advice but sometimes they just wanted to feel her recovery, let it flow into them. Kelly didn't mind; she loved her stories, her recovery, her hope and her love of The Mill and AA and NA. Kelly helped whom she could but she didn't do the work for anyone; she knew they had to experience it themselves. Kelly was enjoying being the voice of the residents and she was now comfortable speaking to staff about what she wanted and what the residents thought they needed. Kelly could see how far she'd come, she knew most of all, because she hadn't needed to listen to Amy in over two weeks. She might tonight and tomorrow, because tomorrow Phoebe was taking her to Sam's memorial service in Plymouth.

Goodbye to Sam

There had been a funeral for family a couple of days ago. The memorial service was organised for people who knew Sam but didn't know the family. It had been organised by The Manor and was designed to help their residents to get some sort of closure, a fellow peer dying is hard to take in. It's not hard to accept a fellow user dying; that happens, addicts die and using goes on. Recovery is different. People live in recovery, they are healthy, they are brimming full of life; Sam certainly was. The service was in a church near the centre of Plymouth. Kelly had bought a black dress and had borrowed a little black jacket. It just didn't feel right. Sam was too young, too lovely, too alive, but unfortunately Sam was too vulnerable.

The church was cold and big and when Kelly and Phoebe arrived only a few people were sat inside. There was a gorgeous picture of Sam smiling and looking so wonderfully happy at the front of the church. As they sat down there was an order of service with the same picture on the front. Some thoughtful words from the manager at The Manor, a beautiful quote from Rumi, "*Wherever a beautiful soul has been, there is a trail of beautiful memories*". The music selected was Angel — Sarah McLachlan and Over the Rainbow — Eva Cassidy and a lovely poem by Joyce Grenfell — Life Goes On.

Kelly couldn't help but think that Sam would've loved it: the poem, the words, the music, the photo — it was all so lovely, not as lovely as Sam actually being here, but lovely. Kelly couldn't remember the service, she heard Sarah McLachlan start singing and then she cried. It seemed to come from her toes. Thankfully, Phoebe had suggested not to wear any makeup in case of tears. Kelly tried to look around through the tears but all she could see was Sam being her friend and she could feel them holding hands. The service was over. Kelly didn't want to speak to anyone, and Phoebe understood it was time to go back to The Mill. Amy was waiting in the car and started singing as soon as they pulled away from the church. Rehab was an appropriate song to start the journey. Kelly felt pretty raw and Phoebe understood. Phoebe's suggestion that Kelly went to the meeting tonight seemed harsh. Kelly wanted to stay in her room and cry curled up in her pyjamas, nestled in the safety of her bed. The thing about being in recovery, though, is that Kelly listened to advice and surprisingly, going to the meeting was a good idea. Firstly, Kyle was there and that made Kelly warm inside and she shared at the meeting about her loss and grief and talking about it made it easier. People related, and people hugged her, and people cared. This really was becoming her fellowship; it felt like family, or at least what Kelly thought family should feel like. The sad thing for Kelly was no one else seemed to know Sam; she hadn't touched that many lives, maybe she hadn't been the Sam she'd known for long enough and the Sam she hadn't known had been like the Kelly she was trying to forget.

Moving On

It was time for Kelly's completion ceremony. Everyone sat in a big circle, Phoebe and Cathy either side of Kelly. Kelly was crying already. There was a giant cake behind her, chocolate and cream and berries and love; the cakes always contained love. Kelly had wanted to complete on the same day as aftercare so Kyle could be here, but it hadn't worked out that way. She got the keys to her flat a day late, but it was her flat, no addicts or alcoholics to share with, no one to trash it, no one to ruin it, it was just hers. Phoebe started to talk. Kelly had arrived a mess, a bundle of need but had become a woman of purpose, a beacon of hope and an anchor for many of her peers. The amount of change in Kelly had been a surprise to everyone; not many people get recovery this much in three months, but the magic about Kelly was she never got in the way, she let recovery in and embraced it with every fibre of her being. Everyone seemed to love Kelly. She was like everyone's favourite sister; they would all miss Kelly. The words of love flowed around the table; the stories of Kelly's compassion, patience and sense of wonder were regaled through happy tears. They all went outside by The Mill wheel for Kelly's photo. Kelly had written some words of thanks for the staff and her friends, but she couldn't read through the tears. She just smiled, her eyes gleamed through the tears and she hugged everyone from her heart. Kelly didn't have a taxi.

Summer arrived to take her to Westfront to her flat. Summer had pulled in some favours to furnish it and kit out the kitchen. She'd also managed to fill up the fridge and freezer with a grant from a local charity. Summer hugged Kelly; Kelly was a wreck. Her peers had bought her a card, and a book of Mindfulness and a great big bunch of flowers. Everyone was hugging and crying as Kelly got into Summer's car. As they drove away leaving the clapping and cheering and crying behind Amy sang her heart out to commemorate the occasion. Kelly had completed something, not just anything, though — she'd completed rehab. Kelly's flat was small, more a studio apartment than a flat, but everything Kelly needed, well, nearly everything. What Kelly's flat needed was a boyfriend and he was coming around soon. Kelly was excited about her flat and excited about her boyfriend. Kyle wasn't coming around until late afternoon for tea and then to go to the NA meeting. They'd planned a day together tomorrow and Kelly was going to make a cake and a special dinner. She didn't have a lot of money but the kitchen had been stocked with some basics by Summer, so Kelly just needed some beef and some herbs and she had everything for a beef bourguignon; that and a cake should be enough for a recovery and completing rehab celebration.

Kelly had an hour to nip into town and get supplies for tea and dinner tomorrow. She didn't need much but she was all jingly inside and couldn't really concentrate, so some fresh air and a gentle wander around the shops was just what she needed. Westfront was still busy with tourists, so an hour went very quickly but Kelly was home, her home, her flat, just her living there, nobody else. She opened her front door and danced into her flat. It was already starting to fill with happiness. She'd only just unpacked the shopping when the doorbell rang. She ran to the door and opened it to an enormous bunch of flowers and a smiling Kyle.

"Come in, come and see my flat, and thanks for the lovely flowers, they are for me, aren't they?"

"Of course, they're for you, it's a flat-warming present."

They kissed and hugged and tried not to squash the flowers.

They went into the kitchenette and Kelly put the unsquashed flowers in a vase; there actually was a glass vase left in the flat and the flowers were lovely. She made them coffee and then they quickly walked around the flat before sitting in the lounge. Kelly couldn't relax at all; she got up and started making tea, ham, egg, chips and beans, and whilst the tea was cooking, she got on with preparing the cake. Kelly was never that good in the kitchen but she learnt a lot at The Mill; the main thing was the confidence to just do it. Kyle was a bit lost; he wasn't much help in the kitchen, but Kelly didn't want any help, she wanted to make tea and dinner tomorrow. Kyle liked it better when he was in control. Kyle set the table and just watched Kelly being happy as she faffed beautifully around her little kitchen. Tea was ready. Kelly had Amy on, she had everything in her flat she needed. Kyle enjoyed tea. He liked a meal that was made for him, he appreciated it most of the time, he knew how much effort Kelly put into everything, he appreciated Kelly. He washed up and they were ready to head off to NA. It wasn't far to walk. They chatted and alternated between holding hands and being arm in arm, but they stayed very close to each other physically and emotionally, happy in each other's space. The meeting was OK, nothing great, Kyle shared about being happy and how his life was very different now; he didn't give much away, he never did, but he said enough to appear authentic to most.

Kyle walked Kelly home. She'd had a perfect day, she loved it all, life now was loveable, Kelly was actually living the dream. Kyle was OK, not enough joy, strong feelings were happening but only the first time made an impression; life in recovery was just drifting. Time with Kelly was special but tonight he was home alone.

Kelly was up and showered by 08:00. Kyle was coming around to take her out to brunch and then it was back to her place for a movie on Kyle's laptop, dinner and then whatever happened next. Kelly had picked up a lovely flowing summer dress in a charity shop whilst out one day at The Mill. Today was the perfect occasion; she wanted to look good, but casual. Kyle would be in his customary jeans, dark coloured tee shirt and dark brown leather jacket, but Kelly wanted to wear a dress, though. Kelly finished the cake, she'd made a dark chocolate and raspberry and cream cake, and it looked great; you couldn't see all the love flowing out of the cake, but Kelly knew it was there.

Kyle got out the shower and thought he'd wear trousers and a shirt today. He normally wore jeans and a tee shirt but today he wanted to look smart. He really liked Kelly and he thought he'd make an effort. He had a coffee, strong and black, an expensive tin of americano instant, easy to make, the right taste every time. He got dressed; he only had one pair of chinos and a couple of shirts, so not much choice, just the idea of being smart, that was choice enough. Kyle had seen the print of Amy in a shop window and he just had to buy it. He knew

Kelly loved Amy and he wanted to get her an actual house-warming present. It was already framed in a silver metal frame and he bought some wrapping paper to make it a proper gift. Kyle had spent some time choosing films and had narrowed it down to a choice of three: *Elizabethtown*, *Stranger than Fiction* and *About Time*. They were very different but great films and Kyle didn't mind which one, he'd chosen the best three he could think of and Kelly could choose which one to watch. Kyle grabbed his jacket, his toothbrush, his laptop, and the films and he hummed the tune to Tempted by Squeeze as this reminded him of the lyrics. He put the wrapped picture under his arm, then headed off to Kelly's. It wasn't like Kyle, but he felt a little nervous. It was fifteen minutes' walk and although Kyle disliked whistling, this feeling was how he imagined people felt when they whistled, that happy on the inside feeling, that they wanted to make a happy noise outside as well. Kyle just sang "Drops of Jupiter" in his head; that way he got to add to his happy feeling without anyone else hearing about it.

Kyle knocked on the door. Kelly opened it immediately; she must have been waiting with her hand on the handle.

"Wow, you look amazing, I've never seen you in girl clothes," said Kyle and stood back to take in the sight.

As he stepped back Kelly said, "You brush up pretty well too, I didn't know you had smart clothes."

They hugged, not a rehab hug, a more intimate type of hug, a boyfriend and girlfriend hug. They kissed too, a sort of more for later type kiss, then made their way inside. Kyle handed over the gift and Kelly unwrapped it as if she had never had a gift before, and then she looked at Amy and cried.

"It's perfect, thanks."

Amy was singing now as Kelly walked around her flat deciding where Amy was going to live; it was hard for Kelly to decide as she couldn't see too well through teary eyes.

"Let's put Amy somewhere later. I'm starving, and brunch is calling. OK Kyle, let's go; Amy can wait."

They wandered off towards the park to find somewhere for brunch. The park in Westfront had a lovely café, and although it was probably going to be busy, it was worth waiting as long as it wasn't too long, as they were both hungry. Kelly felt very different walking around in a dress holding hands with a smartly dressed man; it wasn't long ago that it was so very different. There was room in the café; they sat down, ordered coffee, juice and brunch. Brunch was basically breakfast with chips, just what they wanted; it was the perfect start to the weekend. They were going to stay in tonight. It was an AA meeting and Kelly preferred NA. Kyle didn't really care; he preferred staying in. Conversation was easy; it was mostly about Kelly, but Kelly didn't notice or mind. Kyle listened and paid attention, and for Kelly that was special. It seemed like a few seconds had passed when their brunch arrived, but they had already been there forty-five minutes. They ate and chatted, chatted, held hands, then chatted some more. Drank more coffee without noticing that over three hours had passed. Kyle paid, they left to walk arm in arm around the park. The park was full of summer sounds and smells and people; neither Kyle nor Kelly wanted people around them so just instinctively headed back to Kelly's for movie afternoon. Kelly had bought some popcorn and some pop, a vintage bottle of dandelion and burdock, so she just had to choose which film to watch when they got back. Kelly wasn't bothered which. She just wanted to sit on her sofa in her flat with her boyfriend, watch a film before they had a dinner at her table in her flat with her boyfriend; the rest was just detail. Kelly chose *About Time*. It was partly set in Cornwall and she kind of liked Bill Nighy. She wished he'd been her dad or even her uncle; her life would've been so different to have someone as lovely as Bill Nighy as your dad.

They snuggled on the sofa and were gently entertained by the lovely story so beautifully woven throughout the film. As afternoons go, it was a good one; as days go, it was a good one. Kelly cried at all the emotional bits and Kyle sort of laughed at how easily she cried but inside he liked it. He didn't get tearful like that, he didn't really understand why someone cried, he could follow the plot but it didn't touch him, not on that level; he got the humour, knew when it was sad but no tears, no feelings, nothing more than a superficial touch. He liked the film, though, and he was enjoying Kelly's emotions flowing out of her. The film finished and Kelly clapped, no embarrassment, just joyful clapping. Kyle joined in, clapping the day more than the film.

Kelly got up to start getting the dinner ready to serve. The beef bourguignon was gently simmering, the new potatoes and green beans were nearly ready, so Kelly started to set the table, knives and forks, she opened the cupboard for glasses and the bottle of burgundy was there looking at her, she'd bought it for the recipe and not even noticed as she poured it into the pan with the beef.

"Kyle, I put red wine in the meal and the bottle's here," she said waving the bottle in the air to show Kyle. Kyle smiled; this was more like it. He'd had enough of going without things he liked. Recovery was all right for getting well, but he was well now, and he liked drink and drugs and the freedom to use what he wanted when he wanted it.

"Let's finish it with dinner, no harm done — it's only one bottle."

Dinner was gorgeous. Maybe the wine helped, maybe it added a touch of risk, but the food was great. They chatted freely, both feeling more like a couple than they had before. There was a sense of expectation that tonight was important, their relationship was moving forward. Kyle got up and kissed Kelly, a follow on from the kiss earlier, but this time they both felt something stir; tonight, was going to be the night.

"That was lovely, thank you, the best meal I've had in ages."

Kelly smiled. "What, better than the ham, egg and chips last night?"

Kyle smiled; Kelly loved that smile. "Just, only just, though." Kyle rummaged around his laptop bag and pulled out a small bag. "I've bought us some gear, Kelly, I thought it would be the perfect end to our day."

Kelly didn't want to wait until the end of the day. She wanted it now, she loved heroin: it felt so great, it was perfect, it wasn't something to wait for; heroin was just what she wanted, it was what went with heroin she hated. The lifestyle. The sordid people, the squalor. This wasn't sordid, this was lovely. Beef bourguignon. A lovely flat. A great boyfriend, this was the life she wanted, if she could have a nice bottle of red and heroin to top it all off, then why not?

Kyle never got too excited about injecting. He just liked it; it was the right feeling, a feeling he understood, a calm control he found to be authentic, no artificial crap that recovery was full of, calm and in control. Kyle didn't do the danger and risks of using — that wasn't for him; control and calm in his own environment, in his own way, but this was what he wanted, being with someone, using with someone. He drifted off gentle and calm.

She was ready now but this time she was tingling all over excited like the first time, under the fire escape at the care home, a frightened girl, full of anticipation, full of hatred, full of anger, full of desperation, shame, guilt, sorrow; no, this wasn't like the first time at all, but excited, tingly, alive. She found the vein, easy this time, detox and rehab for four months had made her veins impatient; they wanted it now, they presented themselves, ready for the injection, full of calm. Then she twitched and then nothing; Kelly was gone.

Kyle came around slowly. He always felt a little uncomfortable when he came around. Today was no different, but it was different because Kelly was here; they could feel uncomfortable together. Kelly was still slumped on the sofa.

"Come on, Kelly, get up, let's go out." Kyle walked over to her. "Come on." He nudged her. She fell to the floor, stayed there. Kyle went to help her up, but she was cold, not moving, not breathing, not living. Dead. Kyle stood and looked at what was left of Kelly, he'd loved her but his skin was tingling, he was high, his whole body feeling out of control, his brain buzzing, overconnected, almost overloading, high like he'd never been high before. He was getting off on her being dead, the idea that she'd died, he liked that idea, he wanted that idea, he wanted to be there when someone died, he'd missed it with Kelly, he was crashed on heroin, but next time he'd watch.

Kyle was dancing and singing in his head, Drops of Jupiter, the lyrics loud and clear in his head. Kyle had to get a grip. He needed to leave and not be here. He couldn't clean away his being here — the dinner, the drinks — but could he clear away his part of the drugs and just leave it like Kelly relapsed on her own? He'd close the door, leave, find out about Kelly when everyone else did. He looked back at Kelly, he felt something he hadn't felt in a long time; he couldn't quite tell what it was, but he had a rough idea: it was adrenalin surging through him, it felt like excitement. Kyle walked out of Kelly's flat working hard at not skipping, he kept his head down and avoided CCTVs. He knew what the time was, and he wanted to be away from here, somewhere else. He went via a chemist and bought some codeine linctus, enough to put some morphine in his blood, in case he got tested; he didn't want to show he'd taken heroin. He headed home. He might need to lie low for a while. Kyle thought it might be a good time to visit Mary. He couldn't normally put up with her and her family, but under the circumstances he was prepared to compromise.

Mary

Mary and Jim lived in Bristol, well just outside on the M4 side. They had two boys, Lawrence and Neville, aged eight and twelve. Mary was proud of the life she'd built with Jim. Jim was a good man, not her first love but the man she wanted to spend her life with, hardworking, safe, a great dad and her rock. More often than not the voice of reason and a good sound partner; she pretty much knew where she was with Jim. She remembered the time when she first saw Jim. He was one of the better runners at the club in Swindon that she'd gone to, to recapture the fitness she had at university. Jim was quiet, but confident and was popular at the club, he was slightly older than her, but Mary wasn't bothered about that; she'd had enough of people her age, she wanted a grown up in her life. Jim was an accountant when they met but was now a finance officer at a housing association and they lived in a lovely house and had a very enviable life.

Mary loved her life but, that was the trouble — there was a but. Mary didn't run anymore, she ran about for Lorro and Nev and made sure they were at swimming, cricket, rugby and most recently with Lorro sailing, but she didn't have time for more. Jim didn't run either. He rarely got home from work before seven and by the time they'd eaten it was wine o'clock and then time to sit down and get ready for tomorrow. Life was more than she'd dreamed it would be but at nearly forty she wanted some excitement, or the idea that at some stage soon there'd be some excitement. Which is why she liked Kyle; he was hard work, but he wasn't predictable. He wasn't like other people; he was a really interesting kid brother and he certainly wasn't like Jim, which is why he caused a few problems between her and Jim. Jim didn't like Kyle. Kyle had a terrible work ethic, and an unfounded sense of entitlement, and no respect for Jim, or what Jim did or what Jim had, so perhaps Mary should've asked Jim before she'd said Kyle could come and stay for a few days, but really it was no big deal, they had a spare room. Jim and the kids would be out all day and Mary only worked mornings at the dentist's where she did admin and occasionally covered reception; it wasn't what she'd planned on doing when she got a 2:1 in History at Swindon Uni. That all seemed so long ago now, the work, the studying, the fun, the friendships, the dreams and in all honesty the disappointment.

After graduation she worked at Pizza Express and that job went on too long. She never really applied for many graduate jobs after the initial lack of interviews. Working at Pizza Express had given her time to look after Mum, as Dad was struggling, then she'd met Jim and his career was taking off, then they got married, bought a house, had Lorro, then it all seemed like her choices were made for her.

There'd been some great holidays and she had some lovely friends and Jim's family were smashing, although it was always such a trek up to Ayr; Jim's parents were too old to travel now. Having Kyle round for a few days would be fun. And if he was actually off the drugs, he could be good company, well for her and the boys; they adored Uncle Kyle, maybe because he was the interesting one. So, Jim would just have to put up with him.

Kyle was arriving tomorrow, which gave Jim time to stop sulking. He'd been cross when Mary told him, he'd said he was cross at not being asked, but he was cross that Kyle was coming. He hoped he wouldn't stay long. Jim was thinking how he could get rid of him. Kyle always wanted something, maybe he could just give in easily, get him what he wanted and then wave goodbye. He just had to not be too keen or too obvious; then Mary wouldn't be upset with him. Jim knew that Mary really liked Kyle and that she wanted more of him in her life and the lives of their boys. She felt he added something to their perspective on life, something that was missing here in their settled, normal, quiet, boring life. Jim offered to pick Kyle up from the station as a peace offering. It would give him time to find out what Kyle wanted and earn him some brownie points for playing nice.

Kyle was arriving at 12:20 into Bristol Temple Meads and the plan was for him to stay an undetermined amount of time, which, as far as Jim was concerned, was going to be too long; one day was too long and sometimes just one meal was too long. Jim couldn't help it — he just didn't like Kyle, who he was, what he did, or how he did it. He didn't mind until he started doing it all in his house and in his presence. He practised biting his lip on the way over to the station. He'd get there early; at least then he wouldn't get stressed worrying about being late. That was another thing about Kyle — he didn't ever seem to get stressed.

Jim did get stressed, more than he should. He wasn't fifty yet and he'd already had a couple of heart scares. He couldn't help worrying, the job was too much, the financial responsibility was just too much sometimes. It was such big numbers; if he made a mistake, if anyone made a mistake, he felt liable. He had a department of sixty people who according to his job description actually worked for him. Jim didn't like the drive through Bristol. Traffic just didn't seem to flow right through the city and he found the run into the station quite edgy, more nervy than dangerous but at times it was definitely dangerous; the family car was great when going out at the weekend but not when you wanted a bit of acceleration on a busy roundabout and all you got was safety, economy and comfort, whilst being carved up and getting the finger.

Jim got to the station with about ten minutes to spare, enough time to be early but not enough for a coffee, no bad thing because Jim was drinking too much coffee now, sometimes fifteen cups a day; he'd stopped using the Costa card as he was embarrassed at how many free coffees he was getting, not free on his heart, though. Not using the card made him feel less stressed; anything that lessened the stress was a good thing even if it wasn't real. Jim didn't actually think that pretending he was drinking less coffee was good for his heart.

Jim stood by his car and tried to enjoy the summer sunshine on his skin, feeling the warmth on his forehead that had more skin than hair nowadays. He saw Kyle walking out of the station carrying a small holdall, and a swagger, not as tall as he'd previously thought. Maybe the small holdall meant he wasn't staying long. Kyle spotted Jim and waved, walked over to Jim's car and extended his hand, the friendly handshake. Jim wished he had a firmer grip; Kyle's was manly, strong, sort of authoritative, sort of annoying but then most things about Kyle were annoying. At least Kyle wasn't as tall as Jim remembered.

Jim smiled and in his friendliest voice said, "Hi Kyle, pleased you could come, let's get you back to the house, I think Mary's prepared some lunch."

Kyle looked put out, distant, but Jim remembered he could never trust Kyle's looks. Jim could read people at work, he could always read Mary, but Kyle was like a foreign language, or more alien, or a different species, completely unreadable. Kyle's face twisted into an unrecognisable look.

"Thanks, Jim, I'm looking forward to seeing Mary."

Mary was worried about Jim picking Kyle up. She hoped they'd play nice, she knew they didn't get on but maybe this time, now Kyle was clean, Jim could make a bit more effort. She turned the radio up. It was the song about Moses the cat and the trailer by the sea; she liked that one — Kyle was like Jessie, always a pain in the arse, but boy could he sell a dream.

She was making lunch, a cold meat platter, she'd made coleslaw, potato salad and put together an arbitrary green salad. She knew Kyle wouldn't touch it, but she liked the balance on the table. Mary heard the car pull up, so they must've behaved themselves a little or they'd never have got back so quick.

Kyle was first through the door and threw his arms around Mary. "Hi, sis, you look great." Mary smiled all over, she loved a compliment, especially from Kyle.

"You look pretty good yourself, Kyle, great to see you."

Jim stood back and watched. He could taste the falseness coming off Kyle; Mary was so easily fooled. Jim had been unable to find out what Kyle wanted. Kyle was getting better at reading Jim and could easily parry his probings; perhaps

Kyle would show his hand now. They all sat down at the table, Kyle reached over to grab a plate and said, “Great spread, sis,” and started grabbing meat with his fingers and then a forkful of potato salad. “Did you make this for me?”

Mary loved it. Kyle was great to be around, so thoughtful and kind, even though she knew he wanted something she couldn’t help herself. “Not just for you, but kind of yes.”

“And the coleslaw?”

“Of course.”

Jim could almost be sick. It was like two teenagers flirting, unaware of their friends looking on, unfazed by the giggles and tuts. Mary and Kyle were far too close for brother and sister, well as far as Jim was concerned, they were. Lunch was more flirting and small talk, Kyle avoiding direct questions, presenting his story in pieces, controlling the information that he allowed out, NA, recovery, no drugs, his flat, the lovely crockery they’d bought. Not much about that girl Kelly, he’d barely mentioned her, no surprise to Jim or Mary. Girls never stayed in his life for long. His initial charm was beguiling and interesting but not enduring; most people tired of him. Maybe Kelly just got bored of him; Jim was bored of him. Kyle dropped his first hint. The meetings were great for his recovery, but they were mostly a long way away from Westfront, public transport made attending his four meetings a week really difficult, he could do with a car. What Jim heard there was: boring, boring, boring, can you buy me a car? Jim thought about that: two thousand, maybe three, and then he’d be gone, to Jim that seemed like a bargain. Jim didn’t need to consult Mary. This played into his need to play nice and try harder.

“What sort of car are you hoping to get, Kyle?”

Kyle wanted to be careful here, he hadn't actually wanted to get into this with Jim; he thought he'd have a better chance with Mary when Jim was at work. Jim understood numbers and finances and was less likely to spend as much or anything.

"Oh Jim, I've not been thinking about getting a car, I've got no money, I was just saying it would be easier if I had one."

Jim smiled; he didn't normally enjoy anything about Kyle being in his house, but this could be fun. "We've got a bit of money put away. I'm sure Mary wouldn't mind if we used some to help you out, especially if it helped you get to your important NA meetings." Jim knew that sounded patronising, but he didn't care. He wanted some value from his money; even though it was Mary's inheritance he viewed all their money as his money.

Kyle couldn't always pick up on conversational nuances, but he got all of that from Jim. It wasn't really subtle and consequently it was easy to read. Kyle thought, if that's how it is, he could probably push for five thousand and a year's insurance.

"Well, Jim, I'd like something reliable; you know what the roads in Cornwall are like and something economical, I'm a bit short of money as you know."

"We could go to the Car Shop warehouse in Swindon tomorrow and hopefully get you sorted with something."

Mary had hoped they were going to have a family day out tomorrow, couldn't car shopping wait? Kyle actually picked up on Mary's vibe and offered, "Perhaps we could have an early start and head off to Westonbirt on the way?"

Mary loved Westonbirt. They'd been there a few times when she and Kyle were young, and Jim and the kids liked it as well. She wasn't sure Lorro and Nev would be that keen on an early start but they both liked Uncle Kyle and the chance of eating brunch out always got their attention.

That had been the main event. Jim had gone back to work, an extended lunch meant he'd be home late which left the dining room free for Kyle and Mary to catch up and just chat about whatever Kyle would let the conversation fall on. Mary asked about Kelly, but Kyle kept moving the conversation away, back to Mary and Nev and Lorro. It was like family tennis but without any points being scored, just really long rallies that didn't go anywhere — they looked interesting at first but then they were just dull. Kyle was only interesting for short periods of time, and Mary hadn't done interesting in years.

Kyle said, "I could do with a meeting. There's an NA meeting at 7:00 tonight at the Sally Army near Cabot Circus. I just need a lift there."

Mary thought that Kyle being out this evening would be a great idea, she knew Jim didn't want the boys around Kyle for too long. Mary nodded. "I can get you to the meeting, but you might need a taxi back."

"Thanks Mary, I'll get back somehow."

Mary dropped Kyle in Bristol at 6:30 and gave him £20 for the taxi fare back just in case he needed it. Kyle happily accepted the lift and the cash and wandered off slowly towards the Sally Army building. He didn't need to ask for directions, he recognised the bunch of recovering people outside, smoking roll ups and chatting, about the same things they chatted about in Westfront; there were just more of them in Bristol. Kyle introduced himself and joined the group, he let them know he was up from Cornwall and might be in town for a few days. A bit of banter, a couple of friendly handshakes and a couple of hugs and Kyle was invited to meetings for the next few days. The NA crowd were friendly and welcoming wherever he'd been. All he needed now was a lift home and he'd have £20 to spend on Nev and Lorro tomorrow. Everyone started to pile into the building, upstairs, to a large room, maybe 40-50 people were in already with people still arriving. The chair started the meeting at bang on 7:00 and welcomed Kyle from Cornwall and anyone else who was visiting and then the meeting went like all the others Kyle had attended, until Joli got up and started speaking.

Joli

Joli was the main share. She was stunning, her real name was Jhanvi but she couldn't remember the last time anyone had used it. Her family had disowned her since the details of her drug problem came out. Unfortunately, it was quite public and very embarrassing for an Asian family still working hard at balancing the difficulties of being accepted with social climbing. She lost her job in the city after using at a company party, she went too far. Whilst she thought getting naked and dancing with the boss was just good fun, the boss's wife hadn't seen the funny side. Her manager was left with little choice but to let her go. The drug binge that followed had lasted six days. She eventually woke up in a squat with everything apart from her dress stolen. Her diamond earrings had actually been ripped out leaving her with very sore, torn and bloody lobes. She must've looked a right state when she walked into her apartment block as the concierge insisted on her going to hospital. She got her spare key, went up to her apartment and had a shower. No matter how hard she scrubbed she couldn't wash away the idea of what had happened over the last few days. It was there, in the shower, that she committed to going to rehab, no more; she had plenty left to lose and she didn't like the idea of reaching rock bottom.

Kyle couldn't stop looking at her, her brown eyes, her cropped black hair, her stature. The way she held herself was fantastic. She was alluring, she spoke with intelligence, she was articulate, funny and touching. Her share told the story of her collapse from glory as a top city PR agent to a desperate drug addict who'd sunk to her rock bottom, waking up in a drug den, violated and robbed. Joli was crying again, reduced to tears by her dreadful choices, Kyle was transfixed by her story; she had them all in her hands, holding on to her every word. Kyle was captivated, he had to have her. Kyle wasn't normally interested by anyone at NA but Joli ticked all his boxes and then some. Joli wasn't the vulnerable recovering addict he thought he was looking for, but she was absolutely irresistible.

Kyle shared, he gave his usual non-committal talk about being clean and struggling, no money and family still not trusting him, it's not fair, one day at a time. He added how friendly everyone here in Bristol was and he was looking forward to going to other meetings over the next few days. After the meeting he tried to get to talk to Joli but everyone was talking about her share, people kept coming up to him, being nice, that nice that he had to accept a lift back to Mary's from one of the many helpful people. Dave lived just a few minutes from Mary but was leaving now. Kyle hoped he'd meet Joli at another Bristol meeting before he had to leave for Cornwall. Not that he had anything to get home for, but nobody else knew that yet.

Joli went home to Clifton. She had a very beautiful apartment in a house she owned; it was mortgage free and full of interesting tenants whom she knew and managed with a loose hand. Her interest was piqued by the guy at NA in the shabby brown leather jacket, not that much that she could remember his name. He wasn't the usual recovering addict, though, too much confidence, the swagger in his manner and voice. He might have problems but Joli guessed they were exaggerated and shared for effect, but he had something a little j'ne sais quoi, some charm, some. She wasn't sure but she hadn't been interested in anyone for a while. She hoped he'd be at another meeting this week.

The car

Mary was still up when Kyle got in. Jim was in his study, avoiding him. He was pretending to be working on important spreadsheets but actually playing solitaire. He'd searched online for cars and he'd found a 2013 Hyundai i20 for £4,500 with two years warranty at Swindon Car Shop. Jim could tax it, fill it full of petrol and insure Kyle to drive it away from Bristol and still have change from £5,000. As far as Jim was concerned that was a total bargain. Jim smiled — even Kyle had to feel a tinge of embarrassment at accepting all that.

The trip to Westonbirt had seemed like a great idea and Nev and Lorro were off on some kind of adventure that didn't involve adults. They were so great together; Mary couldn't help feeling proud when she watched them run off. They'd been briefed before they went that they had to leave by four, so they could be at the Car Shop before five o clock. Jim had paid for the car, organised the insurance already and was walking hand in hand with Mary thinking what it would feel like to have his house back. The arboretum was spectacular, an incredible visual display that looked totally different to the last time Jim and Mary had visited. Kyle couldn't remember it at all. They walked and chatted. Jim tagged along feeling smug.

The morning passed quickly. It seemed as if they'd walked miles when they got to a café for brunch. The boys turned up just after they sat down, and everyone had enjoyed the morning. Kyle went into the toilet and on the way back saw a couple of volunteers drinking coffee and eating cake. Amazingly, one of them was the stunning woman from the meeting last night. Kyle knew he had to be careful because anonymity was important, but he couldn't pass up the chance of speaking. Lady luck was running his way, because the other volunteer got up and walked inside. Kyle walked over and introduced himself.

"Hi, my name is Kyle, I saw you at the meeting last night, great share."

Joli smiled. Her whole face shone. "Hi Kyle, my name's Joli, I saw you as well, not like the usual crew."

"I've never been that usual. You don't seem like the usual crew either."

Joli quite liked Kyle. He seemed interesting, different, not like most recovering addicts she met, in fact not like most people she'd met since moving to Bristol.

Joli explained how she volunteered here to help her get in touch with nature and to stop her from getting bored and high whilst she wasn't working. Kyle told her how he was visiting his sister and he pointed over towards where they were sitting.

"That's my sister Mary and her family, Jim, Lorro and Nev." He told her about living in Westfront and volunteering at the gardening project. Then Joli's volunteering colleague returned.

Joli said. "Are you going to the meeting tonight?"

"Yes, I'm just going to pick up a car, so I'm mobile."

Joli smiled again. Kyle thought he'd never tire of that smile. She'd obviously never done methadone; her teeth were perfect and brilliant white, her face was perfect, her figure was pretty perfect too, she was intelligent and apparently single. "OK Kyle, do you want to pick me up at six thirty, we can go and meet together?"

They swapped phone numbers and Joli texted Kyle her address, then she got up and walked off with her colleague.

"See you later then, Kyle," and then that delicious smile.

Kyle went back to join Mary, Jim and the boys, just as their brunch was arriving. "That was Joli from the meeting last night, we're going together tonight to the meeting in Brislington."

Mary liked the commitment to NA that Kyle was showing; this was definitely new. Maybe rehab really had been a good idea. Family brunch, this was what Mary came for, Kyle and Jim being civil, the boys tired and hungry from their adventures and her, surrounded by all that was good in her life, sunshine, brunch, family. When it was like this, she didn't want more, this was plenty, her heart was full. Kyle was impatient, edgy, he wanted to go and get the car and then to meet Joli, but he knew he had to keep on behaving or Jim could easily change his mind. At this point Kyle didn't know that Jim had already bought and insured the car. Jim knew he had something over Kyle and was thoroughly enjoying the control. He always found controlling Kyle difficult, in fact controlling Mary was quite difficult, which was why he kept such a tight rein on the finances. That, he could control, he understood money and numbers flowed easily through his head, he always knew what the financial position was and where the money had gone. Mary couldn't spend more than £10.00 without him knowing, and asking her about it, making her feel as if she should've asked first or shouldn't have spent it at all. He could spend £5,000 and not talk to her. She knew that was the way it was, and it was never spoken about, well not anymore, not after the last time, when he made her feel like shit. But that was a long time ago.

The car was OK. Jim was happy, he could already see Kyle driving back to Cornwall in it. Mary thought it was lovely, not as sporty as she'd imagined, but she could see Kyle visiting much more often in this. Kyle thought it was OK, he wondered what Jim thought the debt was. Kyle didn't mind taking from people, especially Jim, he just didn't like owing anything in return. Kyle said, "I'm not sure, Jim, isn't it a bit too expensive?"

Kyle was pretty sure by now that Jim had already bought it. There now ensued a ridiculous negotiation which ended in Jim giving away any hold he had on Kyle and insisting that it was just a gesture to help him out in his recovery. Kyle did his best to appear gracious as the keys were handed over. Kyle followed them back for a victory tea before he drove off to pick up Joli. Mary had made some sandwiches to go with the meat platter, salad left over from yesterday. It looked as if she'd made a lot of effort as by the time everyone got to the table the spread looked amazing. Kyle was pleased with the car. It drove lovely and although he couldn't get his phone to interact with the music system and play Train, there was a Cranberries CD in the car and Delores was always great to listen to, so the drive back had been great, free car, free music, free insurance and free from emotional blackmail.

"Thanks, Jim, the car is fantastic, it'll get me to lots of meetings and, well it'll get me everywhere."

Jim smiled, feeling slightly beaten by the whole process. "You're welcome, Kyle. I hope you get a lot out of it." What he'd wanted to say was: now piss off back to Cornwall, you scrounging scumbag, but he somehow managed to not use his inside voice. Mary was very happy, she loved helping Kyle and normally Jim wasn't this generous; something must be going right. Lorro was thinking that in a couple of years' time, he'd get Uncle Kyle to help him get a car; it seemed pretty easy for Uncle Kyle.

Kyle headed off to Clifton. He didn't really know that part of Bristol but now it didn't matter. He entered the postcode and the satnav would do the rest. Kyle had never had one before and he could see how helpful they were, no more maps, no more knowing where you were, or knowing the way, just technology in control, he'd just point and steer. Kyle was early, but only by five minutes. Joli was sat outside on the steps, looking amazing; jeans and a jumper and boots weren't supposed to look that good on anyone. Kyle pulled up next to her, well sort of double parked as close as he could and leant over and opened the door. "Nice wheels" and that smile; as she got in, she leant over and kissed his cheek, she smelt expensively delicious. Kyle caught his breath.

Kyle had programmed the satnav with the meeting information, and they drove off to the Cranberries. It wasn't awkward but it was more difficult than Kyle had hoped. Kyle didn't like all the questions Joli asked, he didn't like talking about himself, he kept trying to change to talk about Joli but she was quick and clever and whilst he was driving a still unfamiliar car, she easily outwitted him in the don't talk about yourself game. Although uncomfortable, Kyle was enjoying the verbal fencing, and he thought back to Joli's share and realised she shared like he did — enough information, not too personal, people could empathise and interpret their own way, but the details weren't there. This was getting more interesting. Joli was certainly smarter than your average recovering addict and much kinder on the eyes. Joli was getting into this, she wasn't that bothered about Kyle but the way he played with her intellectually delighted her. She parried and probed whilst he squirmed and countered, an intriguing game of cat and mouse. The journey to the meeting revealed very little about Kyle or Joli apart from that they were crafty and secretive whilst trying to appear open and empathic. Had she met her match? Joli wondered about Kyle, the first time she'd wondered about anyone from NA. She might even invite him in later, but there was no rush. The meeting was dull, just NA people talking about how it had been, and the problems addiction had caused and why now life was different. Some people never tired of the stories and the relating and the empathy and the hugs and the coffee afterwards. If only life was simply coffee and hugs, it would all be so lovely. They said their goodbyes and got into Kyle's shiny silver car and accompanied by the Cranberries again headed back to Clifton. Joli was more relaxed on the drive back, controlled the small talk about the people at the meeting and kept the pace gently flowing about nothing to do with her. Kyle noticed but didn't mind. His phone had just buzzed with a text; he didn't give his number to many people, so he was distracted by the idea of who would be texting him at this time.

When he pulled up at Joli's he said he needed to check his phone. It was a text from Cathy at The Mill. *"Kelly's been found, OD come home."* Kyle wasn't sure but he might've turned a little white, definitely grey.

"Joli, I've got to go home, a friend from rehab's just been found, she'd OD'd."

Joli understood. Too many people died from drugs and alcohol and most of them didn't have family and NA and AA was all they had. She looked at Kyle and tempered her smile. "Sorry, come back and see me when you've said goodbye, maybe I'll invite you in next time." She leant over and kissed him on the cheek again. Kyle enjoyed breathing her in. Joli got out the car and waved, full smile this time, she knew.

Kyle drove back to his sister's, the Cranberries still singing the same songs, Delores seeming to have a knowing lilt to her voice. Kyle parked the car, walked back into the house. Mary was still up. Kyle just showed her the text. "I've got to go back, I'll get up early, I'll be back mid-morning, there's not a lot I can do, but I need to be there or at least I think I do."

Kelly is Gone

Kyle was driving down the M5 thinking about what to say, who to say it to and why to say it. Wondering who found her, how it happened, he was the only one who knew what happened, but he couldn't tell anyone. He planned to go home first, then phone Cathy and see if he could get some information, find out what? Well, just find out. He drove into Westfront and realised for the first time how having a car and living on the main street didn't fit seamlessly together. There was no parking near home, so he drove round again, went up a side street and parked five minutes' walk away. He made his ritualistic coffee, at least that was consistent, listened to Train. He'd phone Cathy soon, now he'd just relax, let Train take control. Kyle had The Mill on his phone and pressed dial. Cathy answered; he recognised her voice.

"Hi Cathy, it's Kyle."

"Oh Kyle, it's terrible, she's dead, she'd relapsed and used. The police found her yesterday, someone from NA called it in, they hadn't seen her. Where were you?"

"I was at my sister's, Mary's near Bristol. Kelly and I had dinner on Saturday, we had some wine, then I went home, I felt a bit bad really, a little relapse."

"Well it looked like Kelly felt worse and then had a proper relapse. Will you organise the funeral, Kyle, you were the closest thing to family that Kelly had? Come in and talk to me, Kyle, we'll help as well."

"OK, Cathy, I'll be around after lunch if that's OK?"

"See you then, Kyle, I'm sorry."

Kyle thought about what he'd just agreed to. It seemed like a big deal now, but at the moment he was full of adrenalin and definitely not thinking clearly. He'd wait until he got back from The Mill before he did anything else.

Kyle had been back to The Mill a couple of times for after care, but he wasn't a regular. It felt weird driving into the car park, walking through the gate to the office, like visiting his old school. He knocked. Cathy opened the door, looking like very school teachery, but then she hugged him. Kyle could feel her crying. Phoebe hugged him next; she was crying too. There was a queue of residents waiting to cry and hug Kyle. Everybody had loved Kelly; hugging Kyle was the closest they could get to hugging Kelly. Cathy explained that The Mill wanted to commission a memorial garden for Kelly and wondered if Kyle had any ideas.

"We didn't really know much about plants and trees. We just liked walking in the park and the gardens," offered Kyle.

Cathy had spoken to Summer and they had made contact with an undertaker in Westfront and had agreed to pay for a small service at the crematorium and a special ashes service at the memorial garden at The Mill. Kyle was OK with that but felt he wanted to do some organising as well. They agreed to meet at the undertaker's on Friday.

Friday came around too quickly and Summer and Phoebe were waiting outside the undertaker's looking somewhat forlorn. Bright clothes covered sad insides. Both Phoebe and Summer had been doing this work for a long time, they knew better than to get attached or involved, but Kelly had been special, she'd been easy to love, hard to remain apart from, she just got inside people, wrapped herself around your heart, no demands, just quick to love. They hugged Kyle again, noticing his detachment, his aloofness, maybe it was his defence mechanism? Maybe he was just a bit cold and unemotional? They went inside and met with Janice. She was the co-ordinator and had a few ideas. Kyle just listened and said, "I can't really take all this in. Can I email things through?"

Janice was fine with that and a date was set for the service, next Thursday, that seemed to give everyone enough time, and they all left. Kyle was pleased to be away, he could feel his shield slipping and he didn't want Summer or Phoebe asking too many, or any questions, for that matter. He was in his car and away before Phoebe had the chance to say anything else. Summer never liked Kyle and wasn't too bothered he'd gone.

Kyle spent the next few days talking to people, listening to music, reading poems and phoning people from NA and AA. He'd been amazed at the feelings for Kelly; his only conclusion was that everybody loved her. He'd planned the service, liaised with Phoebe and even spoken nicely to Summer. He'd got photos off everyone who had one and organised the car to take Kelly on a tour of Westfront. Taking in the park before heading out to the detox and then The Mill before heading out to the crematorium. Kyle had sent all the photos off to be made into flags which he'd used to line the drive into the crematorium, flags of Kelly smiling, laughing, walking, dancing, being, living and over the doorway he'd hung bunting made from more photos. Amy was singing her goodbyes as people started pouring in, people from The Mill, from Detox, from NA and AA, workers and friends, all fighting back tears or crying or both. Janice was stood at the front as all the seats were taken and people were overflowed outside. Janice couldn't remember the last time she'd seen it so full. Normally when people died from an overdose there weren't many mourners. Kelly must've been some special person.

Amy finished singing Back to Black and Janice asked everyone to be quiet for a minute and just remember Kelly. Kyle moved to the front, he'd written some words to say, to read out, a tribute, a memorial, a goodbye.

If you knew Kelly, you'd seen her eyes, so bright, so shining, dangerous
You'd definitely seen her smile, heart-warming, loving, open,
You must've heard her laugh, delightful, infectious, naughty.
You'd felt her presence, she filled up the space, the room, your life, my life,
If you were touched by her hand, so warm, soft, caring.
She loved Amy, she could listen to Amy all day, all night, whatever her mood, Amy made her better.
She loved coffee, the park, ice cream, with a flake, with everything, life with everything.
She loved breakfast, she loved heroin, she loved me, she loved life.
Kelly, I miss you.

Kyle wanted to cry to show he cared but he didn't know how, he just had a tremble in his voice, a loss of certainty that anyone who knew him would've known that was as close as Kyle got to being emotional.

Summer went up to the front. She hadn't written anything — she just spoke, softly but lovingly.

"I worked with Kelly. She touched my heart, she was a client in a million. I want to help them all but I was compelled to help Kelly. She deserved a start, she deserved so much, she never asked for much, apart from breakfast, and maybe an ice-cream, and to listen to Amy, pretty demanding really. I liked her, I'm not supposed to like clients but I liked Kelly, I couldn't help it, I loved her, I'm definitely not supposed to love clients but the thing is everyone loved Kelly."

And then Summer sat down, then one of the girls from NA walked to the front and said, *"I loved her too"* and she was then followed by a line of sixty people who all said, *"I loved her too."* When everyone had moved back to their seats or standing area, Janice appeared by the front and said let's all say goodbye to Kelly and then Texas started playing "Halo". And Kelly was gone, loving her hadn't been enough.

Everyone went in convoy to The Mill to finish their goodbye to Kelly, they wanted it to last, the service, the goodbye, the memory, the thought of Kelly and that feeling of love. Kyle didn't go to the service at The Mill, he just went home.

Lucy

Lucy was enjoying life in Westfront. The buzz of recovery and the laid-back community were just what she needed. The move from Brighton had given her a safer life and the people were kind of similar but not quite as out there as the crowd that kept dragging her down in Brighton. Recruitment had been well paid and not what she planned when graduating in Business Management. She was very soon earning £30K plus and her dad helped her buy a house in Hove at some property auction. He could never put right the problems from childhood, even though he knew he never did anything. Lucy would always know, and he'd always know. For five years Lucy worked hard and paid her dad back. There was no way she was going to stay indebted to him any longer than she had to. She hardly went out for five years; all that extra money repaid the debt. Her student years well behind her, Lucy was now a professional living in her own house in suburbia with no mortgage. Commuting daily in her soft top Mini to her high-powered job as a Recruitment Manager.

Nate had been a client, an interesting client, one that she'd initially thought would struggle to get work. He had some charismatic streak that she couldn't ignore and surprisingly employers went for it too as Nate found work quite quickly. It had been a shock when he called into the office on Friday after work and asked Lucy out, sort of as a thank you but a bit more. Lucy hadn't been out with anyone for almost two years, and that had just been a couple of dates and sex. Neither was memorable and Lucy hadn't missed them. Nate was different to what Lucy thought she wanted, a total change and a direction she was mistakenly looking forward to going in.

The first date was fantastic, a meal, too much to drink, a fumble outside Nate's flat and then a drunken stagger up the stairs and into his flat. So began Lucy's fall into drugs and drink and a complete loss of control. Lucy had dabbled in drugs at Uni but it wasn't her thing then really. It was now, though, the first time she injected heroin with Nate. The hit took away everything that was tugging at her mind, that moment after sex just drifting on heroin, not a care in the world, not a thought she didn't like, just floating gently, calmly, freely; it was just lovely. Where did those eighteen months go? After the first year of Nate being in her life, they were both out of work. Nate got Lucy hooked but he got himself hooked too. Heroin had been his hobby before Lucy, not his life; together they were useless, but apart they couldn't function.

It wasn't just drugs at Nate's place — it was drugs everywhere. All the people Lucy and Nate knew were into drugs and not a lot else. Brighton was slowly killing Lucy. Her resolve had gone, in fact most things had gone. If she couldn't smoke it, or inject it, then why did she need it? Now she wasn't working the days drifted by easier when she was wasted. If she didn't do anything, then there was nothing to regret. She didn't bother with Nate as much now, especially as she could get her own gear, she didn't need him anymore. Nate didn't do anything anyway, he'd never really done anything, apart from completely screw up her life. She had to get away.

Today Lucy was going to change, well at least think about change, because she knew that if life went on like this, she didn't have too much of it left. She was a shadow of Lucy, just half the girl she was with double the problems. What she did have left, though, was some money in the bank and a lot of capital in the house. It all started to form into a plan. Simply, Lucy thought, sell the house, go to rehab, buy a house somewhere else that was cheaper to live in but still by the sea, invest the difference in something that paid an income and chill out and enjoy a drug-free life without a care in the world. Getting off heroin was going to be the first thing. She didn't fancy a home detox with Nate and his using buddies calling around every day trying to help.

Thankfully, she hadn't got rid of her laptop, so she googled detox and rehab. How did people manage before Google? It looked like three to four months and three times as many thousands of pounds could have her clean and ready to move on. She didn't need to do any detoxing at home, she could do it all in a residential setting and be supported throughout, if she could sell her house and move, whilst safely ensconced in a cocoon away from Brighton and a shedload of drugs; everything was going to work out fine. She needed to sell her house, otherwise she'd just come back to the same old crazy and that would be a waste of ten thousand pounds and a whole load of hope.

She didn't want to phone the estate agents, she wanted to meet them, she wanted to deal with a proper person, one she could trust. In her mind, she wanted more than just to sell her house, she wanted to sell and move. One thing at a time, though, the agents would be open tomorrow; checking out drug treatment centres was a big step. Maybe she'd get into a chat session with the website she saw earlier and make some progress, and then perhaps a phone call to an agent. Lucy put some soup in the microwave and got a loaf out of the freezer. She was still eating OK when Nate wasn't here; life was better all-round when Nate wasn't here. She went back to her laptop and typed drug rehab near Brighton and a woman popped up on her screen to chat. It didn't take long to book an assessment for next week. Lucy was exhausted and after her soup she crashed on the sofa to watch a film on Netflix and drifted off and missed the film, felt good though.

Over the next few days Lucy met with estate agents, she talked about selling her house and the idea that she might move to Cornwall. She'd had some great trips to Newquay from Uni and although Newquay wasn't a place to live, Cornwall seemed like it might be. The property prices were significantly cheaper than Hove and after talking through the idea with a couple of agents she could afford three properties in Cornwall. Lucy had been referred to a private property consultant who could manage the sale and then find and purchase properties on her behalf. When she met Shona, she trusted her immediately. She knew that because of Shona her plan was possible. Put the house on the market, head off to detox, sell the house, go to rehab, buy a flat or house to live in, buy two more, move her gear down, let Shona finish the furnishings at her place and the two rentals and then finish at rehab and drive down to her new life in Cornwall. Lucy enjoyed the buzz from dealing with people again, but she couldn't believe how tired she was. The process of doing anything was exhausting. She couldn't cook now; she'd phone up for pizza and crash out. Nothing else to do today; the work starts next week.

Lucy and Shona met at a very plush seaside office. Paperwork was signed and hands were shaken and the whole thing took place whilst overlooking Brighton Pier. Shona was going to deal with the solicitors, the sale and the purchase as well as the furnishings and the move; all Lucy had to do was finish rehab and drive to Cornwall. The initial figures looked as if Lucy would be able to buy a small house and two flats in west Cornwall which would give her an income of one thousand a month. Lucy could manage on that for a couple of years or longer if she was careful with her capital. Lucy and Shona relaxed with coffee and biscuits and tried to make small talk after the business was done. Lucy struggled with small talk now, she'd lost the knack, she didn't watch the news and didn't really know much about the world. She'd stopped having opinions; talk was mainly about who had what and how much, what someone had done after having too much. Lucy didn't think Shona wanted to hear about that sort of thing. She managed a few minutes on the weather, and how nice the pier looked and then made go home noises; she needed some heroin and she'd have to get some on the way home.

Shona didn't like Lucy, she didn't particularly like addicts or alcoholics, she couldn't understand how anyone could let that happen in their lives. Lucy was obviously doing well and in control at some stage in her life but now she was just a sad shell of her former glory. A house, a few thousand and a terrible habit, Shona really didn't understand, but 3% of all transactions was going to be twenty-five to thirty thousand which wasn't bad for three, or four weeks' work. She didn't have to like Lucy to do a good job, and if she did her job right,

Brighton was losing an addict and Cornwall was gaining one, even if she was going to be in recovery. Brighton was going to be a better place in Shona's eyes.

Shona wasn't to tell Lucy what was happening until she was in her last two weeks at rehab but she was under pressure to get everything complete in three months and she couldn't start the real work until the end of next week when Lucy was off to The Priory. Shona decided to drive down to Cornwall and search for properties that would be suitable for Lucy. Shona knew some of Cornwall as her aunt lived at St Ives, not the right location for Lucy at all but she'd ask if she could stay for a few days as a base for her house hunting and maybe a few nights on the town flirting with her cousin's surfy friends, no harm mixing business with pleasure and also the chance to catch up with family and as icing on the cake Shona would save on hotel bills.

Lucy was getting just a little excited at her future free from heroin, free from Nate and free from Brighton. She hummed the "A whole new world" tune from Aladdin. A whole new start, no work, no drugs and as far as she could see no downside. She had a place at The Priory in Southampton and that was where her detox would start, and when her rehab was finished, she was moving to Cornwall. She might even change her name and start over, "A new fantastic point of view". The next three days were a blur. She didn't remember letting Nate in or his scummy friends, but she knew she had to get rid of them and book a taxi to the station for her 10:30 train. She had to get them out or Shona would never be able to.

"Come on, guys. Breakfast's on me, let's go to Spoons." Nobody could resist breakfast at Spoons, especially a free one, when you could drink beer, and nobody cared. Lucy cared but she wanted her house empty, she wanted to pack and get going but packing wasn't going to happen, she was going to detox with the clothes she was wearing and a credit card, but for now, thankfully they were in a couple of taxis going to Spoons.

Her house empty and locked, she'd ring Shona to change the locks later. The atmosphere in Spoons was lively and livelier now Nate and his cronies had arrived, loud and inconsiderate before the beers, louder and ruder now they were filling up on free beer. Lucy put £100 on the table and walked outside to get a taxi. As far as she was concerned that was a bargain, they were gone from her life and she was gone from Brighton.

The train to Southampton was quiet, the trip uneventful, the time apparently in freefall, Spoons to Southampton in what seemed like just a few minutes. Lucy had spoken to Shona, who'd agreed to change the locks today and ended with a good luck in detox wish. Lucy relaxed; apart from Shona no one knew where she was and even better, no one knew where she was going.

Searching for a High

Kyle didn't stay long at the crematorium, he'd said his piece and he didn't want sympathetic small talk from people he didn't care about, and that was most people. He also didn't want staff from any of the establishments Kelly had been to asking him any difficult questions. She was gone and so was he, into his car and driving back to Westfront. He'd had enough of the Cranberries. They'd been replaced by the Coral, good driving music and a good distraction from the noise in his mind. He could normally quieten the noise but now there was a lot happening in his head and he wasn't sure what to do with it. Joli was spinning around in there, bothering him, distracting him from what he needed to do, although at the moment he didn't know what he needed to do. Maybe he did need to see Joli.

Bristol was far enough away. Kyle wondered whether Joli was vulnerable enough to lead into relapse. Kyle didn't think so, but wouldn't that make it more fun? And the chase, the preparation, the idea of leading Joli into overdose and being able to watch as she died, the thought of that was exhilarating, but he did like Joli and wondered whether he wanted a girlfriend or a victim? He couldn't decide whilst he was down in Cornwall, but he didn't want to stay with Mary and Jim in

Bristol for another day. Joli was lovely but not that lovely. He'd phone her tomorrow. Now he just needed sleep, he decided.

The phone call to Joli had been better than expected. Kyle was a bit clumsy on the phone, but surprisingly, so was Joli, clumsy face to face, but their quick minds gave them time to respond to any interpreted communication errors, with the guise of humour and sarcasm always available to fall back on; not so easy on the phone, though. They both muddled through the phone call as bad as each other and got to the result which was a weekend in Exeter, neutral ground, and the progress they both wanted. They both found each other intriguing, or was it interesting, or maybe challenging but certainly different to who you would normally meet at NA, so for both of them the chase was on. Kyle agreed to buy the meals. Joli said she'd pay for the hotel on Saturday night and they agreed to meet for lunch at Pizza Express at one o'clock.

Kyle was too controlling to just turn up on Saturday. He booked the restaurant for lunch and then decided to head to Exeter a day early so he could get a feel for the city and find somewhere to eat on Saturday night. He'd book into a B & B when he got there and maybe take in a meeting. There was an NA meeting near the station and although he was driving, he knew where the station was. A few nights in Exeter sounded like a decent alternative to a Westfront full of what he didn't want. He even thought about sending Mary a text thanking her and Jim for the car; the car was proving very useful now. He didn't bother, though, in the end, he didn't think they'd get the irony, or Jim certainly wouldn't. Kyle didn't know when he'd next need something. Kyle packed a few clothes, enough for three days, and headed off to Exeter. It was only a two-hour drive but recently Kyle had been feeling tired, so he had to stop at the big services on the way out of Cornwall and shut his eyes for half an hour; sleeping was better than crashing. He wasn't in a rush. He had all afternoon to get there. Kyle knew a B & B just up from the station and for forty pounds he had a room and a full English booked for the morning. He showered and lay on the bed drifting peacefully into the sleep his body craved and his mind was screaming for. Three hours of calm and peace, the first time in weeks, he hoped the noise would stay away, he didn't think it would, but he got dressed and walked into town. He had time for chips and curry sauce before the meeting, He'd not eaten much for a couple of days; the noise in his head was already deafening.

The meeting was in a large room and the usual crew were chatting outside. Kyle walked past saying "hi" but not stopping to chat, he'd heard it all before and wasn't here to chat. Sandra wasn't the main share, but she caught his eye. Her share about losing another friend, not having anyone in her life gave Kyle the chance to relate his share about losing his brother. He was able to fake the right emotions now as he'd used this story five or six times. The response was just what he wanted; after the meeting Sandra asked him if they could go for a walk and a chat. They sat by the cathedral talking; it looked as if they were talking but really Sandra was talking and Kyle was steering and listening. Sandra was opening up to Kyle, opening up about things she'd kept buried inside for years. Kyle listened and nodded, touched her hand, her arm and listened, occasionally a word about his brother but mostly just listened. Sandra said it was time to go home and they got up holding hands and walked through the city centre. Sandra was tall, and possibly younger than she looked, the years of using taking their toll. Her grip was light, her slim hands felt small as she walked and talked with Kyle. She stopped talking and turned to Kyle looking into his eyes, she reached her head up and she kissed him. He kissed back, he wasn't surprised as her hands wandered over his body. Sandra looked at Kyle and smiled. Her eyes lit up. "Do you want to come in for coffee, and maybe…"

Kyle kissed her again, smiled and replied, "Maybe? What could that be?"

Sandra's flat was clean and small, not much furniture, almost a kitchen diner with a bathroom and a bed. That was all they needed, though; soon they were naked on the bed, exploring each other's bodies, maybe became certain, sex came easy and felt right, they fitted each other instinctively, the moves and timing perfect. It was lovely for Sandra; it was going to plan for Kyle. Now it was over he was grinning and glowing; it was the after-play he'd come for. Gently touching her shoulder, he asked Sandra if she wanted some gear. He smiled and said, "Sex and heroin, they just go together."

Sandra thought hard, logically she didn't want any, but inside she did. She'd been clean for nearly nine months but now that craving, gnawing at her, growing inside her, the most powerful of triggers, sex and heroin, and it had been good sex; beaten by the opportunity Sandra beamed. "Of course, I do."

Kyle went to his bag and took out his kit. Sandra was excited; that tingle of anticipation had been missing from her life. The desperation returning, she had to have it now, why wasn't it ready? She clamoured for it. Kyle passed the needle; she impatiently snatched it from him and found the vein. Kyle watched. She injected and slumped. Was that it, thought Kyle, then she twitched and slumped again. Kyle stood up, grabbed his phone. Drops of Jupiter played as he danced around. "The lyrics to Drops of Jupiter playing in his head at the bottom of Sandra's bed. He checked her pulse, her body for signs of life, for signs of Sandra. He got dressed and left. Sandra was gone, Kyle was alive, not tired now, electricity surging through his veins; watching was so much more than just being there. Sex and heroin, sex and death, Kyle walked back to the B & B pulling the hoodie up over his head keeping his head down and not looking up at any cameras; he'd been doing that most of the evening, whenever he could, he was buzzing; it was hard to contain. His body didn't want to hide it, he wanted to dance and scream and shout, but that would have to wait until the B & B. Maybe the screaming and shouting would have to wait until he was on the beach, though. He could dance his heart out, if he had one.

The B & B was dull and quiet. His room was large and cold but not a dance floor. The atmosphere wasn't party, it was more let's not celebrate let's just sleep, and be ready for breakfast, which is what a B & B is about. Not the base for solitary celebrations, but no harm in a little dance. Whilst dancing Kyle went over what happened in his head. Sandra's end, that's what happened. Had he left a trail that linked him to her? He thought about the meeting and leaving together, chatting by the cathedral He didn't think anyone had noticed him entering or leaving Sandra's flat. Even if they did, he just had sex and left. What happened next, that was the thing, what happened next was the thing he wanted again, the thrill was already leaving his body, the memories were already less electric and Train was playing in his head, Kyle laughed; the feelings, so like the lyrics. The next morning breakfast was fantastic, a proper full English, with fried bread. Kyle just loved English cuisine fried bread; you couldn't make it up, but the grease from breakfast seemed to soak up his nostalgic reflections of a beautiful evening and his musings of the weekend with Joli.

A Weekend Off

Joli booked the Southernhay Hotel. It was meant to impress and charged accordingly. Joli didn't mind the price. Luxury was mostly missing from her life and so was excitement, sex and fun. Joli thought that Kyle could help with most of the list. She thought of what to pack and that tingle of excitement that hadn't been there for a long time. Her "have fun" music was playing on her expensive music system, exactly what was needed for Right Said Fred and she was starting to feel "Too Sexy" as she packed her little black dress, her red leather jacket and her red shoes. She'd need to make sure they weren't walking too far; they weren't her walking shoes. She packed some other sensible clothes and her trainers, silk pyjamas that she had no intention of wearing. Kyle had got into her head. She hadn't had anyone in there for quite some time. It was quite nice having someone in there again, but as of now she wasn't sure what to do with it, where it was going and why it was there at all. Hopefully the black dress and red shoes would help her find out, that and her smile. She knew that worked, she certainly knew it worked on Kyle, but what if she didn't need the smile?

Kyle left his car at the B & B and went into the city centre to get something to wear for tonight as well as to find somewhere to eat so he'd have somewhere to wear the new clothes he was going to buy. The shops in Exeter were much better than Westfront. Pretty much anywhere was better than Westfront. Kyle liked what he was seeing. Trousers and a shirt from a really nice boutique-style shop that managed to stay on the right side of pretentious. Kyle really liked an olive leather jacket in the window of what looked like an upmarket department store, Kyle thought it was grey; it went well with the blue trousers and the white shirt. A few yards down from the department store Kyle spotted tan, brogue-style boots in a shoe shop that were a must. Opposite the shop was what looked like a very good Turkish restaurant. The day seemed to be going exactly to plan. A new outfit that Kyle felt he looked great in and dinner booked at a stylish restaurant. Everything was set for an excellent weekend. Kyle thought about getting a present for Joli, but he'd no idea what to get; he didn't know that much about her and he didn't want to get something wrong. He fell on the side of get nothing, do no harm. He could maybe tell her later he thought about getting a gift but wasn't sure what to get. He started thinking himself into a hole, how had Joli managed to do that to him? He must more than like her.

Joli got off the train in Exeter and got a taxi to the hotel. She needed to shower and change before lunch. She was planning on underdressing for lunch so the evening outfit would have more effect, and she wasn't sure what the afternoon would bring, hopefully the chance to walk off lunch to make room for dinner. The room was fantastic, almost a suite but not quite, certainly a big room with a great feeling of space and a lot of luxury. The first tick off Joli's list, luxury, she needed more luxury in her life. She hadn't spoilt herself in a long time, the lack of girlfriends and family in her life meant she just got through, she'd stopped having fun, having me time, recovery had become getting by. She wanted more, she sensed that more was coming, bring it on.

Kyle waited outside Pizza Express, nervous, anxious. He didn't know how to do either. In control, uncaring, that was more his style, what was he supposed to do with wet palms? Wait patiently, that was what he was supposed to do. He expected Joli to be fashionably late, but he wanted her to be here now. His inner addict causing him conflict, I want to wait, I want it now, where is it, that and bloody sweaty palms. Is this what Joli was going to do to him? Obviously, it was, and he hadn't even seen that smile yet, where was she?

Joli walked from the hotel, time to get some air, gather her thoughts, calm the butterflies, who put those there, she felt like a schoolgirl, giddy and excited. It was a first date with Kyle, not Ryan Reynolds. She should be able to control herself better than this. Control was normally easy, no, not easy — that implies that it requires some work. Control was effortless, instinctive, almost reflexive, but not today. Out of control seemed to be what was happening. The weather was good, and the sunshine warmed her skin as she slowed her walk down, to bring herself back to in control. She had him if she could take her time, use her smile, pull him in, take what she wanted, use him, manipulate him into what she wanted, have some fun, maybe take him along for the ride, but not get giddy and excited, what were those feelings useful for?

Kyle saw her walking slowly down the road, why so slowly, she must know she's late? He couldn't help but smile, that sort of quirky lopsided smile that he hated, the one that said happy and anxious, not the message he wanted to convey.

She hadn't seen him yet, change the smile, go for pleased to see you smile, not teenage over-excited, stupid look smile. Normally he could control his looks, no, he didn't normally need to — if he wanted a look, he normally forced it, composed his features to emulate an emotion, to appear responsive, well- thought out features presented to support the impression he wanted to create. What was happening? He slowed his breathing, controlled his heart rate, brought back some semblance of control; that was better, more like him; he put on his fake integrity smile, he waved, the over-excited teenager, stupid look, smile, reappeared.

Joli crossed the road, out of the sun into the shade and got to about 400 yards from Pizza Express. She could see Kyle stood on the corner, her heart skipped, she speeded up walking faster, giddier. This was not the plan, slow it down, control the pace, calm outside, calm inside, calm butterflies, stop that bloody flying and flitting about, where has calm gone, smile, he hasn't seen me yet, wave, no not yet, calm, smile. Did she just skip? No, that was a schoolgirl, not her, skipping, she didn't skip, she waved and smiled, and probably skipped.

Kyle waved, through his stupid smile, short breaths, heart rate fast, out of control, sweaty palms, he waved again, he could see her smile, wow.

They didn't knock each other over when they met, they probably over-hugged, to calm each other down, their heart rates slightly out of rhythm found a new rate, more together and slower. They kissed, and politely hugged, held hands and walked into the Pizza Express. They sat outside by the common opposite the cathedral. They didn't talk as much as look at each other and feel the chemistry they generated, the buzz the excitement, the touch, the feeling. They'd waited for this, anticipated this moment, this time together, they now wanted control.

Joli looked across at Kyle, she smiled, her eyes and face shone for all they were worth. “How’s recovery, Kyle?”

Kyle laughed. “Do you fancy wine?”

Joli had guessed right, and then replied, “Just a Rioja and maybe some pizza.” The tone was set, but before they started Kyle said he needed to move the car from the car park to the hotel, a detail he hadn’t planned on, but he couldn’t leave the car there all day, and he didn’t drink and drive. He wasn’t sure why; it was just something he didn’t do. They ordered drinks and pizza and a taxi to Kyle’s car and quickly dealt with the car moving logistics. Joli went along and didn’t ask questions about where or why, although it bothered her; she just went along with the car moving and the getting back to pizza and wine.

They looked across the table at each other and clinked glasses. “To the weekend,” they both said at the same time and laughed. Joli savoured the taste of the wine. She wanted to drink the bottle, but she would control it, easy for now, it hadn’t been easy in the past. It might be easy, it was exciting, a little bit naughty. Recovery was OK but not exciting. Joli missed exciting. Kyle like the wine, he liked the view, he wanted some heroin, he could cope with that want; this weekend wasn’t about heroin — it was about him and Joli. Joli smiled; Kyle knew something was coming but he wasn’t sure what.

“Kyle, let’s get to know each other a bit better this weekend. What if we tell each other two things at lunch and then two more things at dinner, things we couldn’t know about each other, but maybe things we should know.”

Kyle thought, he hadn't planned on revealing too much, but he did want to know more about Joli. "OK, let's see where it goes, sounds interesting."

The pizza arrived and the tables around them had filled with people, mainly couples out for a relaxing lunch, a break from shopping and a host of other reasons, maybe couples like Kyle and Joli, using the time to get to know each other, but probably not playing the same revealing game that they were embarking on.

Joli said, "I'll go first," as she started eating her pizza, smiling and teasing Kyle whilst she toyed with her food, "I lie a lot, I can't help myself. Even when I don't need to, I lie."

Kyle's interest was piqued. "Come on then, give me a couple of examples, you liar."

Joli laughed. "I'm not sure if that would count as one thing then, but I'll tell you one." Joli went on to explain that she lived in a large house in Clifton that she owned. She'd bought it from the money she earnt when working in the city and she lived in the top floor flat. She rented out the rest of the house, which had been converted into three other flats as well as hers. She told her tenants that she rented too and didn't know who the landlord was, she made a reasonable living from the rental income and had an extra lie that she worked from home as a freelance designer.

Kyle was enjoying the wine and pizza and Joli's story. It felt like a proper share, not an NA share; this had some authenticity in it. Kyle said, "OK, my turn, I've got a property-related lie as well. I live in a rented flat that's paid for by Housing Benefit, but I own a flat in Westfront. I got my sister Mary to put it in her name, so I could get rehab paid for and also get benefits. I think that trumps your lie, because mine is a lie and a crime."

A hint of shock in Joli's face, Kyle didn't pick up on that. "Looks like you've raised the stakes, Kyle, but no problem. I think I can keep up. I like to shoplift, clothes mainly. I don't wear them, I just steal them and then give them to charity shops, not to cancel out the bad thing of stealing with a good thing of being charitable, I just don't want the clothes."

Kyle had been listening intently. "I love that, you thieving minx." Kyle wasn't sure what to reveal next. Before he could proceed, they had to decide on whether to order more food and drink or just have coffees. They decided on just the coffee as they both wanted more to eat and drink tonight, enjoy the day, not ruin it by overindulging at the first opportunity.

The coffees arrived and Kyle considered his next reveal. "I don't have a brother, I've never had a brother, but I tell the story of how my brother killed himself after I left him to get caught by the police in a drug den that I took him to. I use the story to relate to people, to help me manipulate people and sometimes just to see how pathetic people are as they react to my story." Joli liked that, she smiled; this was someone to have fun with, someone cold, insensitive, intelligent, a little bit twisted, maybe quite a lot twisted.

"That's a cool story, you're hard, difficult to read, a little unpredictable, a little bit interesting." Somewhat dismissively Joli asked, "What shall we do this afternoon?" Kyle wondered where this was going, this game of truth, this getting to know each other, how much more was there to know? Dinner tonight was going to be interesting. What should they do this afternoon?

They walked down towards the river and hired a canoe at the quay, an afternoon of messing about on the river. Being friends, splashing, being childish, no difficult questions, no emotional fencing, an afternoon off for them both, what they needed, some unwinding fun with a like-minded person. What they'd both been missing in recovery, well it wasn't really recovery anymore, it was more not living like an addict but sort of living like an addict. The two of them doing what they wanted, having what they wanted, not thinking about others, not caring about others, but maybe with a tiny thought for each other, as long as they got their needs met, got their fun, was this becoming what they'd both been looking for?

Joli was drenched. What she was looking for now was a towel. Kyle was wondering if maybe he shouldn't have splashed Joli quite as much. As they returned the canoe to the hire company, Kyle helped Joli out of the canoe, a gentlemanly act that shrouded the mischievous thoughts of drenching her even more. Joli wanted to pull Kyle in but knew he was stronger and could tell he was thinking the same. Joli had to accept she was wetter than Kyle, and that's how it was. The day was long and there'd be chances to win later. No need to try and win everything, a concession now was OK. They walked along the quayside holding hands. Kyle had put his jacket around Joli's shoulders to stop her getting cold and to sort of say sorry, I didn't mean to get you that wet. She wasn't too wet to get in a taxi and they were soon back at the hotel and in the room. Dinner was at seven and they had two hours to kill. Kyle thought he knew exactly what they could do with the time, but Joli wanted to wait until later. She wanted a hot bath and to take her time getting ready to eat. Joli wanted to take her time with Kyle and she also wanted a bath. She walked up to Kyle, grabbed his hands, looked up to his handsome face and kissed him gently, then pulled away and whilst looking up said, "I'm going to have a bath and then get myself ready for our date, see you about six thirty."

She turned and walked to the bathroom, Donna Summer "Love to Love You Baby" playing from her phone. Kyle didn't particularly like it when he didn't get what he wanted, when he wanted it, but he was happy to make allowances for Joli. He was sufficiently interested in what he was going to get later and to accept that he had to wait. He still felt like sulking, though, he'd just keep it to himself.

Summer

Summer had been a recovery worker for five years. She could remember the day as though it was yesterday, coming back to the bedsit and finding Alan dead. He had overdosed on heroin. He'd scored whilst she was out getting food. They'd been together for three years, getting by, using and surviving, not living really, just together, and now he was gone. What was she going to do with the rest of her life? She was going to make sure it didn't have to be that way, that addicts had a choice, that addicts had someone who believed in them. She didn't know how but she was determined. That was the turning point in Summer's life. She went to rehab, then after a couple of years, on to college where she studied to be a drug counsellor. She got a job with SWDP's apprenticeship programme and this eventually led to her role as a community recovery worker. She loved the work, the pay was fine, and she lived in a lovely little house just outside Westfront that she shared with her cat, Merran. Summer liked to meditate and do yoga, things she learnt in rehab, she used them to keep the peace in her life. She didn't have a partner and didn't want one. Merran kept her company and her job kept her busy. Yoga and meditation kept her fit and peaceful. The only problem was she got attached to Kelly. She knew she wasn't supposed to, and her client case load was pretty high, so she shouldn't have the time to get attached, but Kelly slipped through the boundary and got through and now she didn't know what to do. Supervision at work was more about what are you doing and what you can do, rather than how you are you doing and do you need any support emotionally, but Summer didn't need support, she needed to make sure it didn't happen again, she knew addicts would die, she knew the statistics, she just didn't want to be affected by the realities of her job. Some would live and some would die; she just had to keep supporting, keep giving, keep believing and stay unattached. Easy to say, but ever since Kelly died, she had been very attached, thinking what she could've done differently, even though she knew the answer was nothing, asking what more she could've done when she already did more than enough, but with Kelly it wasn't enough.

That was the trouble — it kept coming back to Kelly and Kelly was gone. Summer needed a plan, not one that could help Kelly, unfortunately, but one that could give people like Kelly more chance of making it, more chance of staying alive, less chance of dying. She knew she couldn't do it alone; she already did all she could, but maybe she could start a group that could make some sort of difference. She knew The Mill did aftercare, and SWDP did groups, and NA did meetings, but she knew it wasn't enough. Summer sent out a selective email; she only wanted the right people involved and she didn't want too many people knowing that she'd been affected by a client. She knew the team at The Mill and she knew they'd want to do whatever they could and she thought Lena from detox was someone she could trust; she didn't think her management could help but she needed to present something to them, otherwise it would become a time-consuming hobby and she needed it to be work.

The problem was her manager's response was likely to be a well-meaning well, why don't you just work harder, or that always helpful; why don't you just work through your lunch break and get a few more things done then? Summer found the interchange between her manager and her one of the least helpful strategies for dealing with any of her work problems, so she just kept her head down and got on with stuff. When she had what the company laughably called supervision, she just talked about clients, workload, and how everything was OK. The problem was, it wasn't OK, and she had to do something about it, or it was going to get a lot less OK. More people would die unnecessarily and Summer or some of the other workers were going to get affected.

Lena

Lena loved her job at the detox. It had been a surprise; she did a few cover shifts whilst she was at college studying for a degree in psychology just to help with the bills and she didn't really have a plan to turn those shifts into a career, but cover shifts as a support worker were very different from key working. Now, she got to help people, not faff about cleaning, cooking, driving people to appointments or just doing what everyone else wanted; no, it was very different now, now she helped, now she steered, now she made a proper difference. Lena had just got married and her husband didn't always like that she worked with "junkies and alcoholics". Why couldn't his beautiful wife work in a safe place, with nice people, who weren't going to hurt her if they didn't get what they wanted? They didn't hurt her, though, they were nice people, and it was safe; he just didn't get it. And he was just worried about their baby because Lena was four months pregnant and the baby was starting to show. He didn't want their precious baby hurt, he didn't want his precious wife hurt.

Making a difference was fantastic but to make a difference Lena had to care. She had to believe, and she had to get her clients to believe. Creating that joint vision, that future of hope was what she loved about the job, getting really ill people to start to believe in themselves, to understand that they could have a future without drugs or alcohol or both or one where they weren't controlled by drugs or alcohol. A future full of hope, full of wonder, full of opportunity, Lena believed in that, and she knew that working with community recovery workers and the teams at the rehabs in the South-west she could help to create that future for her clients. It didn't always work, Lena knew that. Some came to detox to get clean so that they could go out and use again, some came to detox to deal, some came because they had to, for court orders or community orders, but some came to detox to change, to start a new life, some came to detox daring to dream and those were the ones she loved to work with. Which is why Sam and Kelly hurt so much. They both got it, they both wanted it, they both needed it and they were both dead. Lena's husband didn't understand, but this was the thing that hurt Lena: the danger was manageable, the risks were obvious, the few that wove their way into her heart — they were the ones that hurt, they were the ones that kept her awake at night, they were the ones she couldn't accept, they were the ones she needed to stop from happening.

She didn't know how, but she knew she had to do something, so there were no more tragic endings for girls like Sam and Kelly. It was OK saying that, but what could she do differently? She knew that her job was about preparing people for change; change came later, when they were substance free, but hope started early. She did hope, detox did hope, detox didn't do enough; somehow, she didn't do enough, well not for Sam and Kelly. Lena committed to doing more. The email from Summer was a good start; she'd definitely meet up and start the conversation, she'd speak to her manager as well, she was OK, she cared, but she couldn't do any more, but she wouldn't block Lena from trying.

Cathy

Cathy was nearing retirement. She'd worked at The Mill for ten years, she'd seen some changes, in the way that The Mill worked and in her life. Her life was lonelier now. Her husband had left and her children had moved on with their lives, leaving her rattling around her house in Westfront. The only thing that hadn't changed was the magnificent view out to sea from all the windows in the front of her house. She never tired of that view; on the difficult days at work, when she got home, it was the view of the Atlantic that recharged her. The waves, the power, sometimes the stillness, but always the ocean. The Mill had changed, the staff team were amazing, always amazing, but now there weren't as many. The cuts in council funding, the years of austerity, just meant less money for staff wages, which translated to less staff, but management and commissioners wanted the same outcomes so she and Phoebe, who were the mainstay of the team, had to work harder. They were good about it, the boundaries were firm, they still went home on time and they always got leave when they wanted it, but they spent less time supporting each other at work, they had less down time at work; it was activity after activity and sometimes after three or four hours of intense client work she just wanted to chat about nothing, relax, go online and look at clothes, not write a report or work at some bloody spreadsheet to demonstrate outcomes.

The clients at The Mill hadn't changed in all her time there. They came with the same problems, the same lies, the same fears and they made the same changes. Some embraced AA and NA and some really, yes really, got the whole Mill thing and even then, the statistics were rubbish. Three out of ten were dead in two years. It didn't seem to matter what they did, thirty percent were here on a death sentence. The only thing that made the job possible, made the job so wonderful, made the job fantastic was that seventy percent were going to live life, they were going to go out into the world, embracing recovery and they were going to run with it.

Cathy never knew who fell into which category and she never knew which ones would fall into her heart. Kelly was one who fell into her heart. Even though Kelly hadn't been her client, she'd been in enough groups and had plenty of input into Kelly's time at The Mill to let her get under her guard. Kelly was so open, so vulnerable, so loveable, so bloody dead. What could she do to stop it happening again? Cathy believed in aftercare and in NA, but there wasn't enough joined up stuff to keep people safe when they left, not a big enough safety net to catch people who'd fell a little bit, to stop them falling all the way, the way she knew so many did. She hoped Summer had an idea, or some sort of plan and that was why she'd emailed. She wanted to do more but didn't know how; they already did so much.

Cathy didn't have long left before she retired and the thought that it had all been a waste nagged at her. She wanted to make a difference, to change the world. And whilst she acknowledged that changing the world was a big ask, she knew that she could change someone's world, and that if she changed enough worlds, on a small scale, then those people would impact the world in a much bigger way and that big problem might have hundreds of tiny solutions. Cathy also thought that God helped. She didn't like to talk about it too much at work — being associated with AA and NA was enough God for most people — but Cathy believed that God had something to do with it, and that ultimately because of that the world would definitely be a better place.

Phoebe

Phoebe had been at The Mill from the beginning. She'd seen it all and been involved in it all. Phoebe thought it unlikely that she could be surprised anymore. She'd had her surprises when she was younger and living the corporate life in London after Uni. Work in media, cocaine and the London music scene were the blur that made up her twenties, but that couldn't last, and something had to give. The thing that gave, though, was Phoebe, and she had a breakdown just before she turned thirty. Recovery was long and hard, both mentally and physically, and she came to Cornwall to be with her elder sister to get her life together.

Diane and Ralph lived on a farm just outside Westfront and they were both absolute rocks for Phoebe just when she needed it. They waited for Phoebe to be ready, they didn't judge, and they never set a timescale. Whilst they waited, they got the builders in and converted one of the barns for Phoebe to live in. As she got gradually better, she slowly moved into her house, which was a beautifully converted three-bedroom barn. By now Steve was a regular around the farm and someone for Phoebe to share her recovery with. Steve was also in recovery. He'd come to Westfront for a new start after an interesting but drug-fuelled life in India. Both Steve and

Phoebe loved the quiet and peace of Westfront and they'd both found the person to share it with. It didn't seem long before the barn was full of family, and when the children were at school Phoebe got a job helping out at The Mill as it started out as a rehab. What began as a part-time job doing everything turned into a job leading the team and shaping the service as it streamlined its way into becoming a modern rehab, not just a local solution for a small part of Cornwall but now a competitive well-run business that majored in recovery. The product was recovery, one of the major tools to recovery was the 12 steps and The Mill worked like a well-oiled machine to get people in early recovery into a life full of hope and supported by AA or NA. Phoebe believed in it. It worked for her and it worked for thousands of other people, as they say in AA, "it works if you work it."

It wasn't complicated; do the suggested things, and it works. Don't, and it doesn't. Phoebe taught that in groups, in one to ones and every passing interaction she had.

When she wasn't working, she sailed her dinghy in the sheltered sea off Westfront and when she wasn't sailing, she was with her family but still thinking about sailing. She didn't think about work when she wasn't at work. She gave people tools to use in their lives to keep recovery. If they used them, they kept recovery; if they didn't, they didn't keep recovery. Phoebe had come to understand that it wasn't her fault what people did with the tools they were given; recovery was a choice and so was relapse. Recovery was better, but people had free will and boy, would they use it.

Phoebe still got to like the occasional client and she was touched by the success stories and saddened by the losses, but she knew it wasn't her fault. She did what she could, she was bloody good at it, but she couldn't do more; she had a family to love and a boat to sail. She also had her own recovery to think about and worrying about other people was no help. She still went to the odd NA meeting, more to keep in touch with what was going on locally than anything else, but NA was still her tribe and she felt she belonged; she was an addict in recovery and that gave her an insight into how addicts thought. She knew when people were faking it and she knew when they wanted it. Phoebe never lost her passion for The Mill and for recovery. It oozed out of every pore of her; she was a part of everything that happened at The Mill and she wanted it to be better, she wanted it to be available to more people and she wanted society to be more understanding and helpful. She wanted to change the world and she wanted to fight all the injustices that people in recovery faced. She thought maybe Summer was on to something, so she was looking forward to finding out more.

Moving to Westfront

Lucy hadn't thought that much about detox. She hadn't thought that much about anything in the last three years; it all just seemed to happen. But at least detox had been a plan, as had Shona and moving away. Where she was going and what life would be like without heroin or drugs and alcohol was the question. Her body seemed to think it would be a lot better, as no drugs and proper meals and sleep seemed to be working wonders with her. She'd had a long conversation with her counsellor about being better and not needing to go through all that rehab business, but she understood the need; detox got rid of the poison in her body and rehab was going to help her change her behaviours so she didn't attract it back in her life. If it all worked properly, she'd have a support team to keep it working and to help her keep her life on track. The time passed quite quickly, and people came and went. Lucy hadn't met any people she cared about, but she had started to care about Lucy. She hadn't heard from Shona, but she wasn't bothered. She didn't need anywhere to live for a few more weeks, and if needed she'd find a hotel for a few weeks. Life was going along just about right for Lucy and she liked not having any worries. Shona could have the hassle for her percentage. Lucy had bought some emotional freedom and she was enjoying it.

Change was easy whilst she didn't have anything to worry about.

Groups about feelings seemed so intense, sharing about feelings had become normal, consequences of drugs might have been painful things to talk about when she arrived, but Lucy got it now. The consequences of using were, well, they were her life. Nate had been a consequence, losing her job had been a consequence, having to sell her house had been a consequence and here she was in rehab, if that wasn't a bloody consequence, what was? She got it: using sucked, and it sucked everything out before it left you emotionally and financially skint. She was lucky, she'd got out early. She still had stuff to lose, but she wasn't going to lose it, she was making these changes to make this life work.

She didn't feel particularly lucky, but she knew she was. She'd met enough people in rehab to know that there was no limit to what you could lose to addiction — family, partners, children, homes, jobs, careers, respect, dignity, hope, health and ultimately life. She was definitely lucky; she still had quite a few things left on that list. She planned to get some back and maybe even add in a few things she didn't have before. Yes, recovery seemed to be bringing opportunities that life before didn't have to offer. She couldn't have known all about it when she first met Nate, but she knew about it now. There was a whole lot more to life than drink and drugs, and that whole lot more added up to what Lucy wanted most. So, bring it on, recovery, let's make it happen.

Shona had been down to her aunt's a couple of times and had chosen Westfront as the place for Lucy to live in. It was well serviced by public transport and had a thriving recovery community. Property was reasonably priced but not cheap and

Lucy could afford a nice house and still have enough for three rental properties as long as Shona shopped around. If Shona did it right, she could furnish Lucy's house with some quality furnishings and the rental properties with a more functional but still quality theme. Shona specialised in doing it right. The sale in Hove was just about to go through and the few tweaks Shona had made to the house had made a real difference to the sale price and the speed it was going through. Shona liked a deadline. It added to the joy she got from making everything happen. So, the trip to her aunt's this time was about making an offer on some properties and maybe closing a couple of deals; that was the buzz, that and meeting the deadline, and delivering over the expectations of the client.

The trip to St Ives proved more successful than Shona had dared to dream. She'd found a lovely cottage on the edge of Westfront that was just perfect for Lucy. It had been empty a while and the family that had inherited were keen to realise the value from their somewhat inconveniently placed asset so they could get on with their lives. This helped Shona get ten thousand off the asking price and shake on the deal. It even had some lovely old furniture in with the price. Shona could mix and match these with some modern pieces and create the look she thought Lucy would go for, deal one done. That was the hardest part over with. Then she'd stumbled across an old semi-detached property that had been converted into two well-sized flats; it didn't need much work and it would be ideal for people on benefits or low incomes.

Shona had researched the area well and knew there was a shortage of property for that target group, so filling the flats with tenants would be easy. The money saved on the first two properties meant that Shona had enough left for a virtually new, two-bed house, in the next village. It was upcoming and local, a perfect rental property for a small family, another group of tenants that struggled to find somewhere reasonably priced to live in west Cornwall. The package that Shona would present to Lucy was a property portfolio with a rental income of £1,350 per month, after agency fees and a lovely cottage to live with no hidden costs to worry about. Shona just needed everything to go to plan back in Brighton and she could say goodbye to Lucy and head off on a well-deserved holiday to Italy. She loved the lifestyle and the food and occasionally the men, but mostly the relaxed laid-back lifestyle. She knew a lovely apartment in Rome that was just perfect as a base.

The deals fell beautifully into place. All the details Shona had insisted on actually happened. *T*s were perfectly crossed and *I*s simultaneously dotted. The Brighton solicitors did a superb job and Shona's money was in the bank, the properties were in Lucy's name and before Shona had moved all the furniture into the cottage the first two tenants were in the flats. Within a week a young family agreed to move into the house but wouldn't be in for a week or two. Shona had done her job and arranged to hand everything over to Lucy in Southampton at the weekend, before flying out to Rome.

Death After Treatment

Lena, Summer, Cathy and Phoebe sat around the office table at The Mill. Phoebe had put *28 Days* on, the film starring Sandra Bullock and showing her journey through rehab. So, the residents would be entertained for 90 minutes, giving them plenty of time to get started. They'd need to finish on time as after the residents had watched the film, Cathy was going to do a debrief. A film like that was full of triggers and things needed to be talked through to keep everyone safe.

Summer started the meeting off by explaining that she wanted it to be low key and without minutes, she wanted everyone to speak freely and hopefully to come up with some radical and out-of-the-box ideas.

Summer was also clear that although her motivation in calling this meeting was the death of Kelly, she didn't want it to be about Kelly but about offering people like Kelly more support at a time of crisis in the hope that a potential death could be prevented.

Summer knew it wasn't something that an individual worker could do, well certainly not a worker at SWDP, and she didn't think that a specific organisation had enough capacity to provide a solution either. Summer was pretty sure that it needed to be a joint venture between as many organisations as possible. Summer felt that, whatever they introduced as a result of their talks, she was pretty sure one session wouldn't be enough. It would need to be delivered consistently to clients, from the beginning of their recovery journey and reinforced at every subsequent meeting. Whatever they decided, they had to be 100% behind it, 100% of the time. Summer also knew that whatever they did, it wouldn't work all the time; nothing did.

Lena wanted to have a phone number that people who relapsed could call. She did shifts at the detox and they got calls at all hours from people who'd relapsed. The problem was the calls were handled differently by different workers, not badly, just differently. But Lena wanted a duty call handler, to take the calls across all services, with an agreed message and an agreed pathway for people to follow, including the person who called and the collective organisation. That way every call could be followed up. The commissioners would need to be involved as if people needed to reengage with services, that would need paying for somehow. Lena felt that this would be a relatively simple process to implement and a card with the number on could be given to everyone who engaged with services. This could then be reinforced at every stage of treatment. Getting the phone number answered was a logistics problem that needed management support across a few organisations, but it wasn't impossible.

Cathy felt it was more about behaviour change, getting people to think before they act rather act, then think. One of the things they promoted at The Mill was personal responsibility and that mattered more when living in the community than when actively in treatment. They gave three questions on a card to people who completed, and they were encouraged to use this before doing everything, and as a second line of defence to be able to discuss the answers with their AA or NA sponsor before they acted.

Is this good for my recovery?
Is this good for me?
What are my intentions behind this?

Cathy knew that if this advice was followed it was fool proof. If nobody did things that weren't good for themselves or their recovery, then nobody would relapse. Cathy felt it much better to work at prevention rather than trying to rescue people after they'd relapsed. To support this argument Cathy read out a poem by Joseph Malins. She knew it from hearing John Denver recite it when she saw one of his concerts on TV.

The poem is called "A Fence or an Ambulance".

'Twas a dangerous cliff, as they freely confessed,
though to walk near its crest was so pleasant;
but over its terrible edge there had slipped
a duke and full many a peasant.

So the people said something would have to be done,
but their projects did not at all tally;
some said, 'Put a fence 'round the edge of the cliff,'
some, 'An ambulance down in the valley.'

But the cry for the ambulance carried the day,
for it spread through the neighboring city;
a fence may be useful or not, it is true, but each heart became
full of pity

for those who slipped over the dangerous cliff;

And the dwellers in highway and alley
gave pounds and gave pence, not to put up a fence,
but an ambulance down in the valley.

'For the cliff is all right, if your careful,' they said,
'and if folks even slip and are dropping,
it isn't the slipping that hurts them so much
as the shock down below when they're stopping.'

So day after day, as these mishaps occurred,
quick forth would those rescuers sally
to pick up the victims who fell off the cliff,
with their ambulance down in the valley.

Then an old sage remarked: 'It's a marvel to me
that people give far more attention
to repairing results than to stopping the cause,
when they'd much better aim at prevention.
Let us stop at its source all this mischief,' cried he,
'come, neighbors and friends, let us rally;
if the cliff we will fence, we might almost dispense
with the ambulance down in the valley.'

by Joseph Malins

Cathy was concerned that they were going to be distracted by the need for an ambulance because people had died, and whilst people dying was horrible, what they needed was a metaphorical fence.

They all loved the poem and felt it was a good time to break for coffee, tea and cake.

A move about, around the grounds, a chance for Summer to have a smoke and a break from thinking about relapse and death. The job was hard enough, and the responsibility sometimes weighed heavy on everyone's shoulders; cake helped. This was a bought cake, completely devoid of love in the ingredient list, lots of sugar and cream and jam, though.

Break over, they sat back down, and Phoebe started to talk but pre-empted her comments with the statement that she didn't want to be controversial but, she knew that the 'but' word undid all the words preceding it, but anyway. "Treatment, as much as we work hard at doing our best, however passionate we are, and whatever we do, might not have any impact on people at all. We do our best, some do OK, some don't, can we do any more, probably not, can we do anything differently? I'm not sure. Would it make any difference if we did, I don't know?

"The one thing we could do is get more people into treatment; then we would touch more lives and give more people the chance. The end result would still be more would die, but more would live. It's just a numbers game, no matter what we do some will, some won't.

"We always have some empty rooms here, and it would be great if we could run at maximum occupancy, with a waiting list; that would mean that we could get 86 completed in a year, whereas now the total is more like 70. Of those 70 we expect about 20 to be dead in a couple of years with 50 doing well in recovery, and if we increased the numbers to 86, the tally would be more like 26 dead with 60 doing well in recovery. If we put all our efforts into getting more people into treatment, we can make a real difference, without changing what we do, just doing it for more people."

Summer wanted to do something and thought that peer champions could be used more. If people had someone to support them in the community, that might give them the lifeline they needed. She knew that they had to be careful using people in early recovery, as they were so vulnerable, but something radical needed to be done and involving peer champions was something that SWDP were doing more, and it was a good way of introducing new workers to the industry.

Summer summed up the ideas they'd discussed and suggested they have an informal talk to management about their meeting and then get together again in two weeks' time. She thanked Cathy and Phoebe for letting them use their office and for providing the cake. Next time she promised to bring the cake. They hugged and said their goodbyes. Getting together had been good, but the problem was frustrating for all of them, and whilst they didn't disagree with any of the ideas that they'd talked about, they didn't actually agree with any of them either. It seemed as if all they'd done was identify a big problem and talked around it for a while, without getting anywhere near solving it.

Lucy — Reflections from Rehab

It hadn't been like *28 days* or *Being Charlie*, but Lucy's time in rehab had been strangely transformative. She'd been disappointed in her peers. Looking back now, Lucy probably had a slight expectation that she'd meet some vulnerable musician or budding actor who was going to find her as he simultaneously found himself and then she was going to be whisked off on the journey of a lifetime that involved nothing but first-class flights and hotels alongside white sandy beaches. Lucy can admit now that those musings were somewhat idealistic and totally unrealistic, but rehab is unrealistic, people do and say unrealistic things, they get vulnerable, they open up, they find things in other people that they didn't know they were looking for and they feel a whole range of feelings that they have been suppressing for years. And they do all the above in the accelerated timescale of about two months. If that's not a recipe for being whisked off on a dream life, then what is?

It wasn't like that for Lucy; maybe that wasn't what she wanted. Lucy enjoyed not finding someone else, she enjoyed the journey of self-discovery she'd been on. Apart from Nate, Lucy hadn't really had a serious relationship since college and when she thought about it, it wasn't that serious either. Her degree was what mattered to her, the assignments, the grades, being the best in class, beating the competition, even though she knew it wasn't a competition, it was to her. That competitive edge had helped her to get that job in recruitment, that single-minded dedication had kept her working and saving so she could pay her dad back. The drive had enabled her to be the youngest manager at her firm, but she never felt satisfied, she didn't value herself, believe she was worth it. She couldn't put it all down to being sexually abused by that bastard of an uncle. It wasn't all her dad's fault for not stopping it either, but they were both massive contributing factors. It wasn't fair, it shouldn't have happened. What she knew now, though, and what she hadn't really known before, was that it wasn't her fault. She had been an innocent child, who blamed herself. She should have been protected, looked after, kept safe. All of her achievements, hard work, the drive, focus, the determination, didn't get her away from those feelings, because they were just there. Ignoring them hadn't worked, ignoring them didn't work. The thing that Lucy found at rehab was the ability to acknowledge her feelings. It was OK to be angry, and being angry was the right response sometimes. If something made her angry, then she could be angry.

That was freedom, freedom from the past; it no longer controlled her, held her back from real feelings, stopped her from experiencing life on her terms. Lucy knew it wasn't that simple. Just being angry every now and then wasn't going to make her life perfect; a bit of anger wasn't going to get her the keys to the city. But being able to healthily express her emotions in the moment was the gift that rehab gave her. Maybe she didn't need whisking off on some Caribbean cruise to find happiness. Maybe, just maybe, happiness was hidden inside her; she just had to start looking and she'd find it. It was in her, not attached to some musician or actor. Nobody else could make her whole; she was the one, two half-people in a relationship didn't make a whole relationship, or as they said in AA, "two sickies don't make welly."

Lucy was getting quite reflective now. Rehab had given her that too. She liked time each day to be contemplative, to sit peacefully in a room, without the noise or interference of other people or the twenty-first century; what a change, no striving, just sitting, thinking, or if she got it right, not thinking. This was what she liked, and she didn't need to be with anyone to achieve it. This was enough, no one else to please, just herself, and in that peaceful place she could learn to like herself. She was setting the bar low to start with; she'd aim for like at first and when that didn't sound too vain, too incongruous, too impossible, then from that point, somewhere in her future, she'd aim for love herself, just thinking it seemed weird, did anyone actually love themselves? Or was it just a chapter heading in a bunch of self-help books that nobody ever bothered to colour in, let alone read. Like yourself, that would do for now.

Lucy had two weeks left. At the weekend Shona was bringing her future to her. Apparently, everything had worked out and she was able to move into her cottage in two weeks' time. Shona was taking her out to lunch. This would be the first grown up thing she'd done in two and a half months. Actually, the first grown up thing she'd done in nearly two years. She'd been out of the grounds of the rehab to town, but it felt like a school outing where you had to hold hands when you crossed the road; keep yourself safe and keep your peers safe had been the doctrine for trips out from rehab. She'd also been out to NA meetings, but they were controlled outings, to controlled settings, full of controlling people. That didn't mean she didn't like NA; she actually did, but most of the time it was presented and controlled, almost stage managed. That was what people needed, the chance to share something with their peers, to talk about their day, their life, to a group of people who got them, who understood them, didn't judge them, cared about them. Which is why people viewed these groups, as a fellowship, a kind of tribe or community that supported, a community that worked. It might be a bit artificial at times, but what wasn't? Lucy hadn't felt it was her fellowship, though, maybe she'd find her fellowship in Cornwall?

Lucy was strangely excited at the idea of going out to lunch with Shona. She'd decided on a dress and her favourite denim jacket, for some reason she wanted to look good. She actually put on makeup. She'd brought it with her but never even considered using it. However, today it seemed appropriate. She cared, but, and this was the but, she didn't like that she cared what Shona thought about her. That was surprisingly shallow for Lucy's new personally developed self; here she was telling herself she was working towards self-actualisation, but then she wanted Shona to appreciate how she looked.

Shona was professionally early and professionally dressed, in a pinstripe skirt suit and heels that made her legs look amazing. Lucy hadn't really noticed Shona's legs before, she hadn't really noticed Shona before, but she did today. They hugged. Lucy felt a charge rush through her, did Shona do that to her? Shona told her how well she looked and offered to drive to lunch. They found a good looking and quiet tapas restaurant.

Lucy thought they were probably early and there before the main lunchtime rush, but it turned out they weren't; it was just quiet, good food and good news.

Shona presented Lucy with her property portfolio. The cottage looked lovely, the old furniture and the new contrasted so well, the décor perfect, the town of Westfront looked quaint. Shona had even found details of NA and AA meetings so Lucy could continue with her recovery and hopefully find a sponsor. The house, converted into flats, looked great and already full of two tenants and the two-bed house with the family moving in. Lucy couldn't believe how fantastic everything had worked out. She wanted to jump up and kiss Shona. That wasn't the only reason she wanted to kiss Shona, though; Lucy felt the first pangs of a crush.

Shona was delighted with the portfolio she'd put together for Lucy. She knew she'd given her the chance to get a new life. Westfront seemed the ideal place to start that life. Shona was pleased to hand everything over, she could move on, head out to Italy for a well-earned break. There'd been just a bit too much pressure this time. It all worked out but there was a point about four weeks ago when it looked as if it was going to go dramatically wrong. Estate agents, solicitors and people, she'd had to do wine and dine too much on this project; maybe next time she'd give herself more time. All this for someone she hadn't liked. Lucy looked much better than Shona remembered; rehab had obviously done her a lot of good. But not just to look at, but she was something to look at, she was interesting, she was attentive, she was good company. Shona hadn't had good company for a while, and she caught herself flirting with Lucy. She'd picked up on that message, the tension in Lucy; it felt as if Lucy was looking at her legs, her mouth, wanting to kiss her. This was a business lunch, though, not two college girls playing with their sexuality, juggling with a girl crush on a whim of self-discovery, no, this was business and tomorrow she was off to Italy.

Lunch and business concluded, they got back into Shona's car and headed back to rehab. Shona thought about lunch and she thought about Lucy and then said, "I'm off to Italy for a break, Lucy, when I'm back why don't I come down to Westfront and see how you're settling in?"

Lucy smiled. She'd wanted to say something but hadn't known how to, so much for knowing how to express her feelings in the moment. Life was great in theory, in the group room, in the artificial atmosphere of rehab, but in real life, in a car with someone you wanted to kiss, someone you wanted to see again, why couldn't it work there?

"That would be lovely, Shona, I'd love it if you came down to see me. I could buy you dinner?"

Shona laughed. "Let's call it a date, then." She'd chosen the words carefully, she wanted it to be a date, but she knew it could be taken the other way. It wasn't.

Lucy giggled and replied, "A date it is then, I'll buy a new dress."

"Me too," said Shona. Shona pulled up at the rehab and they both got out of the car. They stood facing each other.

Lucy picked up both Shona's hands and gazed into Shona's eyes. "Thanks for everything, you've been amazing. I couldn't have done this without your help."

Shona smiled, to hide the tear forming in her eye. "Good luck, and take care," and then Shona leant forward and they kissed. Shona felt that kiss all over her body. Lucy's heart vaulted, what was happening, she hadn't come to rehab to find a property manager, she certainly hadn't come to rehab to find a girl, but what a find, what a feeling, what was she going to do for two whole weeks?

Shona was gone, driving back to Brighton, singing to herself, "I kissed a girl and I liked it." She didn't know enough of the words really but enough to keep herself smiling inside. She more than liked it, she definitely wanted more of it, wanted more of Lucy, Lucy in her new dress, well to be honest Lucy not in her dress, and she wanted Lucy. The trip to Italy was definitely going to drag, well maybe not entirely, but it was going to be a long two weeks.

Two weeks goes very quickly in rehab. Now that Lucy had an address to go to, her key worker was able to arrange for an NA sponsor to meet her in Westfront before she went to her first meeting. Lucy also had her ending session with her key worker. She never really liked Pat; he was OK, he listened well, he nodded at all the right times, he related experiences in the right way, he offered advice at all the appropriate times, he asked about feelings, he helped her personalise things rather than generalise; she simply didn't like him. He was a bit direct, not soft around the edges, just not, well just not, she didn't know, but finishing off with Pat wasn't hard; there was no attachment, no relationship, just something that was over now.

Maybe he'd done a fantastic job and Lucy had done all the work, as she was supposed to, discovered her feelings, let go of her resentments and learnt to be, in a different way because of his support, not in spite of it; it just felt as if she'd done it all because they hadn't connected, not because of his intuitive loose help, more his lack of help. The place itself had been fantastic, the rehab experience, the service, the care, the direction, the groups, the projects, the everything, just not Pat. So, the ending was easy, the goodbye party was still to come.

Party, it's not really a party, but a buffet, with a variety of soft drinks, herbal teas and caffeine-free teas and coffees, with cake; celebration isn't celebration without cake. Lucy didn't really like cake, she loved the small savoury bites in the buffet, but she had some cake, because it was her cake. Pat started the goodbye talk, he said nice things, but not the sort of nice things that someone who really knew you said. It was non-committal, almost impersonal. That was the theme. No one had actually got close to Lucy, not the musician or the actor or the businessmen or the weather woman, none of them, they'd just been there whilst Lucy had got what she wanted, she'd completed and she was off to her new life in Westfront and in a couple of weeks' time her Shona and her legs were coming to see her, in her new dress. She climbed into her Mini and waved to her ex-buddies from rehab, as she started to drive off, not sad, pleased, but not happy; then she remembered: happy was a choice, she could do happy, she wasn't bothered, but she did, whilst she waved, Cornwall here I come.

Dinner and Secrets

A quiet table in the back corner of the restaurant was just perfect. Kyle held Joli's chair out at as she sat down and then sat opposite her. He leant over and held her hand. "You look amazing, beautiful, but more than that, perfect, sexy, fantastic."

Joli smiled. She knew that worked. "You look pretty good yourself, handsome, sort of, and maybe sexy too."

They looked like a very attractive couple and they looked as if they were having a good time. They'd ordered drinks, some water and a bottle of Turkish red to start with, neither of them caring about abstinence. They didn't want to miss out on anything, certainly not a bottle or two of red with dinner. The menu was excellent and there was a lot of choice but after much discussion and a surprising amount of indecision they agreed on sharing some mezze for starters and a platter as a main. The food and drink ordered, the appreciation of each completed at least on the surface, it had reached the time to carry on with their game of disclosure. Kyle leant back, took a deep breath and said. "Well, you started first at lunch, so I should start first this evening."

Joli nodded. "I'm looking forward to your reveals, I wonder, what will I know about you?" Then that smile, Kyle tried to smile back and look cool, but he sort of went for an unintended goofy impression, goofy with sweaty hands, what was that about?

Kyle steadied himself, and then started on his third reveal. “When I was on a sales conference, I had sex with two men. It was the first time I’d ever had sex with men, and really, I don’t know what the fuss is all about. It’s just sex, I’ve not bothered to do it again, gay sex was OK, but I prefer sex with women.”

Joli had been listening intently, trying to stay calm, calm on the outside anyway. Inside her stomach was alternating between backflips and somersaults. Where was that control, she was so good at? “I’m just trying to imagine that, three naked men, were they hot like you?”

“Any more information might count as another reveal,” said Kyle, rather hoping he could get away with telling Joli less about himself.

Joli held his hand. “You don’t have to tell me, I’ll just visualise it for a moment or two and pretend they were hot like you, but that kind of steals my thunder, because my next reveal is similar. I’m bi-sexual, I haven’t decided between boys or girls, it’s just people for me, depending on how I feel at the time. At the moment it’s boys, well boy, well you actually, but who knows?”

Kyle laughed, he liked the playfulness, the toying with roles and with him; this was the perfect accompaniment to an excellent meal. The starters were great and the wine was gone, the second bottle was ordered and Joli was already feeling a little tipsy; she didn’t want to be drunk, but she liked tipsy, that moment just before out of control, that acceleration, the rush, the feeling of invincibility.

"Should I go next?" asked Joli, "Then you can finish off before we get a taxi back to the hotel."

Kyle didn't need to think long. He wasn't sure if he was ready for his next reveal yet. "OK, you go next, what have you got left for me?"

"Right," said Joli, "this needs a bit of setting up. When I was at college, I was one of the cool kids, I don't know how, I just was, confident, attractive, and clever, and one of the boys in the not so cool kids group had a proper crush on me. I played him for weeks, so he was almost following me around like a pet, then one evening, I led him on so much so he asked me out. I agreed to go out that night to a place where all the other cool kids and most of the not so cool kids would be, and to meet at the time when everyone would be there. I went with my friends, the cool kids' group, and when this boy came over to talk to me for our date, I completely ignored him and when he said about our date, I just said he should stop lying to impress people. He was devastated, almost destroyed and he avoided everyone socially for most of the term. The thing is, I loved that feeling of power, the control over him, playing with him in front of my friends, it was a total rush."

"Great story," said Kyle, "and in a way it sets up my last reveal which I have to say I wasn't sure about telling you, but I guess that's the nature of the game, isn't it, we're not shocking each other with war stories of using consequences, we're telling each other what we're like, how we function, what makes us different and what makes us the same." Joli was intrigued as to what Kyle had saved, and even more intriguing, he hadn't been put off her or even flinched at her past and her reveals.

Kyle wasn't sure if Joli was ready for this, he'd have to see, he needed to concentrate, to try to read her face. It was so hard to read, as when he looked at her, he was lost. Those eyes, that smile just went straight through his attempts at analysis; he was like a vulnerable puppy in front of her, but somehow, he was OK with that. So here goes, thought Kyle. "When in rehab, I met a girl, Kelly, I liked her. We liked each other, she cooked me dinner at her flat after rehab, we were kind of on a date. After dinner we had sex, and then we had some heroin. I took it, I'd never really liked being clean, I always felt it was someone else's plan, not mine, so I prepared the heroin. Kelly was desperate for it, we sat up in bed and injected. I just drifted off. It was the best high in years, being clean for a few months certainly clears the body and makes the drugs work better. When I came round, Kelly was dead, she didn't come round." Kyle looked at Joli. She wasn't put off, she wanted more, she was almost slavering with excitement. Kyle couldn't believe it, he carried on. "As I checked that she was dead, I started to get a rush, like the first time I did drugs, a feeling, an electric charge surging through my body, like I imagine I'm going to feel every time I inject but I never do, and then I found myself dancing, to Drops Of Jupiter playing in my head, dancing around the room with Kelly dead on the floor."

Joli grabbed his hands. "Wow, wow, wow, what a story, you callous bastard, I love it, I think I love you, that was amazing, let's go to our room." Kyle couldn't believe how relieved he felt, relieved that she didn't mind, relieved that he'd told someone, just relieved, a bit pissed, a lot happy, and relieved. That had been some game of truth; let's not play that again, thought Kyle.

Joli leant against Kyle in the taxi. His strength felt good against her slightly drunk body. She put her hand on his leg and felt him twitch. She liked that, the sensuous touch, the feeling, they were merging, synching together, she felt it, she liked the chemistry, they were outside the hotel. Laughing and giggling they walked and staggered a little to their room. Once inside they started undressing each other, discarding clothes as they made their way to the bed, no drugs, just sex, discovery, delight and then drunken slumber. They woke up wrapped around each other, happy in each other's arms and legs, touching and feeling, slowly positioning themselves for pre-breakfast sex, the perfect start to their day, the perfect start to their future, the anticipation, the wonder of where this was going, that tingle of electricity through their bodies, they both felt that.

Over breakfast Joli wanted to know more, what did it feel like? Why "Drops of Jupiter"? Were you worried about being caught? Did you care? Would you do it again? Can I come next time? So many questions, so much excitement, that tingling, it just wouldn't go away. She'd always thought she could kill somebody, but now she wanted to, her thoughts were rushing away from her. Where was that control, she used to have? Kyle was trying to be calm, but he was full of adrenalin at the idea of Joli knowing, not minding, wanting to be involved. He didn't know, he couldn't think through the rush, the surge of everything coursing through his mind, blocking out clarity of anything. "Drops of Jupiter is my song," was the best he could do, "the rest we'll have to think about, let's just have breakfast, I need to calm down."

"Me too," said Joli, "but let's not think too long."

Lucy in Westfront

Lucy pulled up outside her cottage. The satnav had brought her through a few lanes that Lucy was sure had to be wrong, but turned out to be main roads just outside Westfront. The cottage, her cottage, looked great, the autumn sun casting shadows over the front walls. Lucy opened the door and stepped inside. Shona had set the boiler to work, so the place felt warm and already just a little bit cosy. The house in Hove had been big, and a good investment, not so much a home, more a business deal, but this, her cottage, there she was again, her cottage, already felt like home. Lucy flitted from room to room, admiring curtains, cushions, tables, chairs, a lovely old dresser, beautifully coordinated room after room. Yes, Lucy was going to love it here.

The fridge was empty, but the kitchen was well stocked, and Shona had booked an online shop delivery for later today with all the perishables Lucy would need. There was a choice of ready meals in the freezer, so time for an early dinner of fish pie, not the stargazy pie that this part of Cornwall was famous for, but the fish pie that came from a freezer in any of the supermarkets, before Lucy was going to meet her sponsor at NA.

They'd spoken on the phone; Nancy had agreed to be a temporary sponsor until they either agreed to make it permanent or to make a change. Lucy was nervous, not about the fish pie but about meeting Nancy and about going to a new NA meeting. Nervous was nice though; Lucy liked it. She'd learnt about anxiety in rehab, and nervousness and how it can be a good thing that certainly doesn't have to be a disabling thing. Her feelings were just her body telling her something was going on, something to notice, something that needed paying attention to. Now thought it was time for fish pie and sparkling water, her first meal in Westfront. She raised her glass to Shona. She'd go dress shopping tomorrow; she'd have someone to wear it for at the weekend.

The meeting was only a ten-minute drive and Lucy parked somewhere near. She didn't know what Nancy looked like, a forty-something with brown hair, she said she'd be wearing an old black leather jacket. Lucy had her denim jacket on, to compliment her nerves; they both knew what they were looking for. They spotted each other and waved. Nancy walked towards Lucy, said hello and hugged; it was NA after all, lots of hugs. Nancy did a few introductions, everyone seemed open and friendly. Not as many people as at meetings in Southampton, but the rehab took fifteen or so, so the numbers were artificially high. This looked intimate in comparison, maybe no more than ten people. Nancy said a few more might come; the numbers were normally between ten and twenty. Lucy didn't mind sharing in front of a few people; sharing in front of a crowd was always a bit more nerve wracking. Lucy was made officially welcome by the chair. Nancy shared, to start with she said she was Lucy's temporary sponsor until she wasn't. Nancy's story was compelling, not a big share, just how she was struggling with letting things go, resentments she knew she shouldn't have, but hey, life's harder in real life than in theory — working the steps was easy to say, sometimes it was hard to live, well not really sometimes, it was hard all the time. The people that made it look easy, they deserved to be resented, well, whilst Nancy was feeling like this they did, and those comments, those people, who were just so annoying, why should she let go of that? Nancy's share was full of humour and incredibly human. Lucy liked her; she'd definitely do as a sponsor. Lucy shared, not much, just hello, she was new in town, she'd just finished rehab, she was a few months clean; she was looking forward to living in Westfront. Making a home here, and she was looking forward to making some friends. More than anything, though, she was looking forward to Shona coming to see her. She didn't share that last bit, she just thought it, felt it, desperately wanted it. After the meeting Lucy and Nancy agreed to meet tomorrow at some café in a park that Lucy would find with technology. Nancy wanted to discuss rehab, get Lucy started on some step work, not just so Nancy could get to know her better, but to give Lucy something to do. Lucy felt she had something to do, she had some shops to visit. This wasn't normally her thing, though; tomorrow she was going to hit the shops of Westfront, after coffee with Nancy.

Lucy went back to her cottage. She greeted it, "Hello house." It still felt warm inside, warm at that thought and as she went inside, she noticed how warm the cottage was as she put her jacket on the stand in the hall. Lucy clattered around her kitchen, looking for something. She wanted a little snack before bed. Something was missing from today; she couldn't put her finger on it, but cheese and biscuits would help, and maybe just a small glass of red, not that she wanted a glass of red — she just couldn't stop thinking about one. In reality it had gone past thinking now, it was obsessing, it was driving her crazy. Nothing else in the world existed apart that glass of wine that didn't bloody exist either. Lucy was thinking about going out to get wine, and maybe some vodka when she managed to find something inside her that wasn't out of control, that wasn't in the grip of a craving gone crazy, and that tiny part of sensible. Lucy managed to phone Nancy. Nancy was great and managed to talk her down, calm her down, stop her going out, talk her through getting ready for bed and into a different mindset. Still chatting to Nancy, Lucy snuggled into bed, feeling just a little bit silly, and feeling very vulnerable. For tonight, feeling that she was OK and in recovery. It was looking like it might be the rollercoaster ride she'd heard talked about at NA meetings and in groups, recovery, why couldn't it be easy?

Lucy found the park and the café and noticed Nancy waiting outside. The autumn air was cold in the shade, but the café had plenty of room inside. Nancy wanted to talk. Lucy wanted the ground to open up and swallow her. She'd only been in town a day and she'd already had to call for help, she didn't feel like the grown-up woman she wanted to be, she was just that lost little girl who needed to be looked after because the horrible things were happening. She cast her mind back to when they were happening, she just admitted to herself she was just lonely, and a little bit lost, but the feelings came back and she just wanted them to go away. Drink helped with that, heroin did that better; thankfully she didn't know where to score here yet. Rehab made her feel more, but rehab didn't stop the cravings. Lucy realised that was her job. Last night it was

Nancy's job. Lucy was embarrassed and ashamed; coffee wasn't helping. Nancy's peaceful, calming and reassuring words didn't help either. Lucy still felt shit and now she was crying, just to add to the embarrassment. Nancy would never want to be her sponsor now.

Nancy put down her coffee cup and started to speak. "That was a big thing you did yesterday, well lots of big things all put together. You turned up at a meeting in a town you didn't know, you met me for the first time, you spoke at a meeting and went home to your new cottage and had a craving. Rather than act on it, you called for help. That's a collection of big things and you should be proud. You started to fight for your recovery. It's not easy but you're not alone, what's the first word in the steps?"

Lucy thought for a moment and then answered, "We."

Nancy nodded. "That's right, we, because it's a we programme, not an I programme, so don't ever be embarrassed or ashamed about asking for help."

Then Nancy got up and walked around the table opening her arms. Lucy understood that; it was time for a hug. She stood up and Nancy hugged her. Lucy hugged back and cried some more. Lucy snorted and spluttered a thank you, wiped her face on a napkin and then sat down and drank coffee trying to smile and not be needy and helpless. Where was the strong woman, she thought she was? Where was her self-respect? Her sense of decency? One day out of rehab and she just felt so useless. Nancy was great, a real tower of strength, but she obviously had something else to do today, other than babysit Lucy.

Lucy said she had some things to do and thanked Nancy for everything. Nancy wanted to stay longer but Lucy was more than insistent. Nancy made Lucy promise to go to the meeting tonight; it was a bit further out of town but not too hard to find. Lucy put the address in her phone, and they hugged again. The tears had finished as they said goodbye, and a not very confident Lucy walked out to go dress shopping.

To say that Westfront isn't blessed with designer boutiques and top end clothes shops would be an understatement. The high street is charity shops, fast food outlets and tourist shops. There were a few shops just off the high street and Lucy did try on three dresses, one of which was acceptable, but not the look she wanted, not what she wanted to be wearing, more likely what she didn't want to be wearing. But she didn't want to just settle for something, so she kept on going. In a side street on the way down to the quayside she found a gorgeous little shop selling local designer clothes and jewellery; it actually had a choice of things to wear that were just perfect. The staff were great, and she was made to feel important, special and like the grown up she wanted. The choice was too hard, so she bought two dresses, one a slightly sexy fitted short black number and a summery, swishy, floral print that she felt very pretty in, and left feeling great, completely different to the wreck she'd been yesterday. Was retail therapy that wholesome or was it just that she'd satisfied the inner addict and got what she'd wanted? What's with all this self-analysis? thought Lucy as she went off to look for her car.

Westfront wasn't that big, but she'd been walking for a couple of hours and not really paying attention. She'd left it somewhere near the park and now she didn't know where her car or the park was. She thought about asking for help, Nancy had said what a good idea that was and she was just by the

Clipper pub; she could pop in there and ask for directions. Lucy knew pubs were not a good idea and right now she didn't want a drink and she certainly didn't want the guilt. Lucy retraced her steps, looking for landmarks she recognised. It didn't take as long as before, as she didn't have to go into the disappointing shops and pretend to like the dull clothes; now she just had to walk and after a short time she was driving home.

Professionals Making a Plan

Summer had made a cake, she knew that the team at The Mill got to eat a lot of homemade cakes, so she'd made a lot of effort to make this cake special; she liked going to The Mill, she liked recovery and it was strong there, it was as if the force ran through the place and Cathy and Phoebe were two recovery Jedis. She knew a lot of people in Westfront put the success of their recovery down to those two amazing women. A joint project was the chance to let some of that Jedi mastery rub off on her. Lena was great too, she did an amazing job at the detox, she just seemed to have an endless source of compassion and patience; these were wonderful superpowers to have in recovery, especially in the early stages. Summer had spoken to her manager and nothing she suggested was in danger of being supported. SWDP had less money than last year and more work, more people wouldn't be funded for treatment but if she wanted to devote her time to a joint project, then management would support her as long as she didn't fall behind in her actual work. This was exactly the sort of response Summer had expected, and exactly why she hated SWDP. It was her job she loved, helping people, finding that spark of hope and fanning it, getting other agencies involved and standing back and watching wonderful things happen, not reporting outcomes or completing risk assessments. She liked to work with people, not systems; systems didn't save people, they just didn't.

Summer put the cake in her car and drove over to The Mill, listening to Amy on the way, her thoughts drifting back to Kelly and why she wanted to do something, to provide just one more thing, to give people in early recovery whatever that thing was; it was better than nothing. If it saved one life, it was worth it, but what would it look like?

Elaine managed The Mill. She had done for six years now and every time she spoke to Cathy or Phoebe she felt as if she wasn't respected or appreciated. She wasn't undermined — they just didn't seem to need her, they did everything, the place ran like clockwork, she just dealt with the marketing, the website, the finances and the board. She wasn't involved in the therapeutic side of what went on and from assessment to completion she had almost nothing to do with residents or staff, so when Phoebe spoke to her about a piece of collaborative work between SWDP, CS Detox and The Mill, Elaine felt it was something she should lead, well if not lead, at least take credit for its success.

As Phoebe talked through the salient points from the first meeting Elaine was interested enough to say she'd come to the next meeting, maybe not all of it, as she was busy with a tender at the moment and a hundred other things, but she'd definitely come. Phoebe knew what that meant. If it was going to cost any money, it would be stopped, unless it looked as if there was good publicity for Elaine and then it would start and then get forgotten, but if it could work well without any additional expense then Elaine wanted the credit for coming up with all the ideas.

Lena hadn't had much support from her manager either as at the detox it was hard to do much more. They weren't dismissive, just not enthused, but it was OK for Lena to keep going. Cathy had left it to be Phoebe to speak to Elaine. Cathy was tired of Elaine now; it was never well done, the mantra just seemed to be: do more with less support and no extra money. It was hard for Cathy to maintain her calm when talking to Elaine, so it was generally easier not to talk to her.

Lena, Cathy and Phoebe were sat around the table chatting about sailing when Summer and the cake arrived, apple and plum sponge. The chat moved from sailing to cake and then to work as the four women talked of their frustrations with management and finances and just the limited vision and compassion of the organisations they worked for. Phoebe explained that Elaine was going to sit in on some of the meeting but that they should start without her. They went over the ideas that they'd discussed previously and the shortfalls that a lack of funding meant to most of them. No chance of funding more placements at rehab, the reality was it was going to be less. Panel decisions were harder, and it was almost impossible to get funding for anyone but the most acute case. People who'd already been through the treatment cycle had had their money and until they ended up in hospital the state didn't have anything for them.

There was no money for a staffed service doing anything other than what they did already. Helplines weren't going to happen, help had to be done during the normal course of treatment not after it, the money wasn't there, and it wouldn't be. All that was left was the idea of recovery champions and prevention, so the discussion moved on to whether these two ideas could be merged into some kind of working plan. It was at this point that Elaine breezed in, wanting to take over, but wanting coffee. “I must have a coffee before I can do anything, I’m a proper coffee addict,” stated Elaine.

Phoebe didn’t even look up. She just replied somewhat nonchalantly, “Have you ever blown anyone for coffee?” No response, just a room full of shock. Phoebe hadn’t finished. “Because if you haven’t blown anyone for coffee then you’re not addicted to it.” She’d finished now, a statement of truth if ever there was one, and a lesson in addictive behaviour for Elaine. This glimpse into Phoebe’s past revealed too much, which was why for Elaine, she didn’t like to get this close to the front line, this close to front line staff and this close to Phoebe.

Elaine was uncomfortable with the harsh reality of addiction, the harsh reality of what they did at The Mill, and Elaine didn’t know what to say; in all fairness, no one knew what to say. Elaine walked over to the cafetière and just poured herself a coffee, no oral sex was involved, she just poured it. She took her coffee and walked out of the office without saying anything, back to the safety of her own office and her tender, which was very important work.

Cathy laughed, but she knew that dealing with Elaine was her job for the rest of the week. Phoebe needed to keep her head down and keep it and the rest of her body away from Elaine. It was funny, though; they giggled through coffee and mouthfuls of apple and plum cake. The good thing about Elaine leaving was that the cake shared more easily between four than five. Lena and Summer were still in a sense of mild shock that had Phoebe really said that? Yes, she had and now she was feeling a little ashamed of herself. Only a little bit mind, she kind of felt that Elaine deserved it — don’t undermine addiction, it was what she did. But now, she was doing coffee and cake and Summer had made a very good cake.

The idea of using service users as recovery champions always sat uncomfortably with Phoebe and Cathy. They were too vulnerable, too keen to be needed, to be the answer, to fall into ego-driven behaviour and become some sort of recovery guru. It was using people at their most vulnerable and the risk was huge. If it went wrong, the risk was death, which added to the problem rather solving it. It was important that whatever they came up with, it was the system that did the saving, not the person. People in early recovery were too quick to help other people, at the expense of themselves. They'd seen it too many times and they didn't want to be responsible for any more unnecessary deaths. However, they felt there was mileage in it somehow; the premise of AA and NA was still one addict helping another and if they could expand on that, then maybe they'd have something they could run with.

They also liked the idea of Cathy's card with the three questions on it, and felt that if they could print out cards with five names and numbers on, people to contact before picking up, a pre-relapse support number, then they just might have a working solution. Finding five people would be easy — everyone would want to help; picking five people would be the hard part. They'd also need to check the numbers regularly and to provide the people with genuine emotional support. There'd need to be a timescale, so people didn't spend too long as pre-relapse supporters, and there'd have to be a pipeline of replacement volunteers. It was starting to sound like a plan; once it was all in place then there would need to be a training programme, everyone involved.

Then it would need promoting and training in rehab and detox so that when people went out into the dangerous world of recovery if they started to feel a craving they'd know who to call, if they incorporated it into their training programme every four weeks no one would miss it, and if cards were given during ending sessions it would be a logical fit. The whole thing wouldn't cost that much, and the extra work was well worth it as they could all see how it could make a proper difference in the lives of people who were at their most vulnerable.

More coffee, the last of the cake, then Cathy offered to convert all their discussions into an action plan and create a working model over the next few weeks. Most of the work would be done at The Mill and once the first few stages were completed, Lena at detox and Summer in the community could start to promote the new service. Summer was delighted. This hadn't just been about coffee and cake and chatting; what they'd come up with was real, and more importantly it could work, it wasn't going to cost much, and its impact could be huge. A good morning's work, and something that she didn't say to herself too often, "That was a really good meeting, I enjoyed it, I contributed to it, the things we agreed on will make a difference, we might just save a life."

The burning question she still had, though, was would this have saved Kelly? She'd never know, and she knew they couldn't save everyone, but she wanted to. As did Cathy, Lena and Phoebe, but one was a good start.

Shona in Rome

Rome was beautiful. The apartment, the location in the Trevi district was perfect, the sunshine, it was warm every day, the atmosphere, relaxed but lively, the food, Shona loved Italian food, the wine, and she loved the wine too, and the people; she hadn't dined alone since she'd been here, different cafés in different piazzas. Shona could manage a few sentences of Italian, more a politeness than a mastery, ordering food and wine, saying hello, some courtesies, and lots of theoretical conversations that worked perfectly until the other person actually started speaking and the words formed into incomprehensible strings, but she smiled and shrugged fluently and people mostly spoke English when she needed.

Shona was relaxed and happy, looking forward to new things when she got home, not anxious about them, just excited. She knew she was giving off some sort of hormonal message of attraction as Greta was the third person to come on to her in as many days. The thing about Greta, though, was that Shona found her utterly irresistible — her dark eyes, her full lips, her Roman face, her elegant body. Everything really, even her job as a lawyer with the World Food Programme, made her fascinating, powerful and sexy. Greta obviously felt the same about Shona as tonight they were dining alone, just off from the group of friends that Shona had been mixing with. Tonight, she and Greta were sharing an intimate dinner, less food, but more wine, more touching, more smiling, more flirting, and Shona was caught up in the romance of the moment. She'd already forgotten about the girl from rehab, now she was with a woman in Rome. They finished dinner and whilst they shared a bottle of Franciacorta, they explored each other as much as was acceptable in a public place, groped is more accurate than explored, and quite a lot of groping is apparently appropriate in Rome.

They giggled and kissed and groped and then stumbled and giggled and groped some more on the way back to Greta's fantastic house. Everything about it was chic, everything about Greta was amazing. Shona was lost in her, lost in the whole Greta experience. The weekend was the best weekend Shona had ever had, the sex was outstanding, the laughter, contagious, the friendship, Shona had to admit this was what she wanted, though the intensity trailed off as the second week started, as Greta had work. Greta had some of the best work outfits. Starting the day with this intelligent, successful, beautiful woman was wonderful, sharing breakfast, the faster pace of the morning, as Greta prepared for work, the softness of Greta, so attentive to Shona as she left for work.

Greta wanted Shona to stay, she'd fallen for Shona, she didn't want to wait, she didn't want a long-distance relationship, she had a busy career, she didn't have time for that to work, but she had time for Shona if she stayed. Her house was plenty big enough. There was room in her house and her life for Shona, but not in Brighton, only in Rome. It wasn't an ultimatum, but if it was, it was the nicest Shona had ever been presented with. It was more a statement of truth, just how it was, how it could, how it couldn't be. The clarity of message wasn't lost on Shona; she wanted to stay as well. Shona hadn't been this happy before, she felt complete. Even if it was a holiday romance, it was worth taking further. She had no work commitments to go back for and she could promote her business with an international slant when she felt ready. Now she could just enjoy life, let it wash over her, Shona had decided. Tonight, she'd let Greta know she was moving in. She wouldn't bother telling Lucy she was moving on. They hadn't been anything but potential. Greta had more potential as well as some realism, some beautiful history, some energy, some love and a very exciting future.

Back in Westfront

Kyle waved goodbye as Joli's train headed off to Bristol, taking Joli with it. He'd had a terrific time with Joli. She was something else, and sure fine-looking, man. The thing is Kyle had almost forgotten about Sandra and that feeling, but he hadn't forgotten about the need for the rush. He constantly craved it; it wouldn't leave him. Talking to Joli had just amplified it, intensified it; he tried to think about Joli and to calm the urges to do OD someone again. To calm the urgency, the pressing nature of addiction, he needed to do it again. For now, he decided he'd drive home to Westfront and just "be" for a day or two. He needed to see Sergei as well, as he needed some gear, not for him (gear didn't come close anymore, it probably never would, not anymore), gear for his next victim, whoever and wherever they were. Westfront suddenly seemed exciting, his life seemed exciting, Joli was exciting, their future looked exhilarating. For an exciting town, though, Westfront still managed to hide on the dull side of boring, not as dull as before, though; now there was some future, a waiting energy to be discovered, to savour and play with. If he understood Joli correctly, this energy was there for them to discover together; now that was exciting, but it was also risky. Kyle didn't think he was taking much risk, just helping somebody go over the edge, assisting their decision to relapse, just a facilitator who took pleasure in his trade, who liked the result as much as the process, not really committing a crime, not even doing something wrong, just reconnecting an addict to their substance of choice, and when he thought about it, in a nice way.

What he'd done hadn't been seedy, it hadn't been forced, it had just been about the pursuit of pleasure, for both parties; his pleasure was just more enduring than theirs. He had to admit he got the most out of it. If there was a winner, it was him, but his burning question now was, could it be Joli as well?

Sergei wasn't difficult to find, but then being a dealer would be really difficult if people couldn't find you. Sergei was loud and obvious. Kyle didn't think he did discreet; his young friend wasn't discreet either. She was off her face on some of Sergei's finest and she didn't care who knew. In her current state she didn't care about much, she wasn't really naked, but she wasn't far off. The early evening patrons of the Clipper didn't mind. She might have been wasted but she was good to look at, sprawled across Sergei showing too much of her skinny abused body. He didn't mind people looking, and if they bought enough gear, he didn't mind what they did. She was just an optional extra for his better customers. As long as they brought her back and carried on buying, he didn't mind. Leather jackets were more important, that and satisfied customers, because after all, Sergei was a businessman, a raconteur and at the moment, he was the person calling the shots.

Kyle just wanted gear, no questions, no extras, just gear, the best quality and enough to not have to see Sergei too regularly. Sergei wanted to chat; Kyle wanted to leave. A beer was the compromise, and a couple of shots of decent vodka. Sergei liked to think he was a simple man who liked simple pleasures, he wanted friendship as well as business, he never managed to get anywhere close with any of his clients, but he could make Kyle have a drink before doing business.

The two men drank beer and clinked vodka glasses and talked about nothing; well, that was Kyle's take on it, nothing he cared about — he just wanted to go. He handed over a thousand pounds, enough for two weeks if he were using regularly, enough for at least three if not four more people. He'd need to see Sergei again in a couple of weeks, so he didn't think he was buying elsewhere, demonstrate some brand loyalty or whatever Sergei wanted to think. As far as Kyle was concerned the less Sergei thought the better. Drinking with Sergei was uncomfortable. He was unpredictable, he knew too much, he said too much. Kyle was starting to think about variables, what was controllable, what wasn't, what linked him to things, which of his movements were traceable, how much of a trail he was leaving. He decided to try and relax, enjoy the beer, the vodka, the moment, the Clipper. A lot of excellent nights out had started at the Clipper, good memories. It was generally only the starts he could remember. Not now, now he was in control, well he would be as soon as he could get away from Sergei.

Kyle paced his flat, a table full of gear staring at him, not craving to use it. He was desperate to use it. It clawed at him, but not how he used to use it; no, this gear wasn't for him, this was for his next victim, for her veins, for her use, for her last trip. Drops of Jupiter played; Kyle couldn't stop pacing, he couldn't stop the craving, the obsessing, his mind racing, no logic, no control. Not the state he wanted to be in. Food, maybe that was the answer, did he have anything in the freezer? He knew he didn't. He'd not made any food here since Kelly. He hadn't even thought about Kelly. She'd been important once, but not now, especially now he didn't have anything in the freezer; he needed to go and buy food.

The supermarket was only a few minutes' drive. He'd go and buy a few days' food to distract him. The gear called to him. Maybe he could take it with him and find someone now, as well as food shop. He knew he couldn't, he knew obsession, he ignored the gear, he could obsess about it when he got back. Kyle couldn't face a full shop, not for everything. This was just about some ready meals; he'd get some cereal and milk as well. That would see him through a few days, give him time to plan his next move, his next, his mind trailed off into a spree of bodies, sprawled over floors, and him dancing, happy, delirious. No Joli, just him and bodies. Where was Joli? Did she fit in this fantasy, in this dream of carnage he could so clearly picture ahead of him? Not now, though, before him now was liver and bacon and sausage and mash, enjoyable, but not the same.

Liver and bacon in the micro-wave and gear on the table. Maybe if he put it away, he wouldn't hear it so much, he wouldn't be as affected by it. He had to wait, take his time, plan his next time carefully, he couldn't leave a trail, he had to be careful. The more he did, the greater the risk. Stop and plan, plan on his own, or with Joli? After dinner, not now, put the gear away, in the bathroom cupboard, everywhere else it would scream at him. He shut the bathroom door. Dinner and planning, dinner and not thinking about killing was the best he could do. Maybe he'd phone Joli after dinner. Maybe she could come down to Westfront? Liver and bacon normally tasted better.

Joli was back in Bristol before her thoughts had settled. Drops of Jupiter, she couldn't stop thinking about it, she wanted to hear it loud, to dance to it, to understand it, to understand Kyle. Joli had downloaded it to her phone, and for a bit of entertainment had set it to be Kyle's ringtone. Now she wanted to dance. The door to her flat closed behind her. She put down her bags and she set up her music to play loud. She danced, she listened to lyrics and she thought about Kyle, but then she thought about what she really craved, not Kyle, but a victim, a helpless, vulnerable victim, the power, the rush, the overwhelming feeling of, Joli couldn't put a word on it, she could feel it, feel it taking over her, but she couldn't name it, she had to feel it, experience it, she couldn't wait, she had to wait, she had to see Kyle; he had the key, the answer.

Joli didn't have any commitments in Bristol, not now. Her commitments were in Cornwall, in Westfront, her commitment was to Kyle. Her phone was ringing. She hadn't noticed, she hadn't noticed anything. It was a missed call from Kyle. She phoned him straight back, she never did that, always poised, always in control, never reactive. This was different, this was exciting; exciting didn't happen often enough.

"Hi Kyle," and then the response was garbled, almost unintelligible, certainly incomprehensible — well, all but the last part. "Of course, I want to come to Westfront. I'll see you this evening, I'll text you the time from the train, see you later." And there was the plan. She didn't unpack, she just grabbed a few more things, put them in another bag and headed out of the door. The bus was quiet, before the afternoon school run, just Joli and her thoughts screaming out loud, no noise getting through from outside, just chaos inside, thoughts of Kyle, dancing, death, overdose. Not just thoughts, feelings trying to explode out of her. Somehow Joli managed to keep her thoughts and feelings inside her and get herself and her inner turmoil on to the train to Westfront. Some tasteless Virgin trains herbal tea was the best choice from the buffet; anything with caffeine was definitely not needed. Chocolate, maybe that would help, wasn't there something in chocolate that calmed the brain? Joli was sure that chocolate increased serotonin production, which reduced stress. There was something to do with flavanols as well, but Joli wasn't sure. Still, chamomile tea, serotonin and flavanols and Joli would soon be calm, with only gentle thoughts to keep her company on the journey to Westfront.

Maybe there just wasn't enough chocolate. A small bar of dark chocolate possibly only had one flavanol in it, and enough serotonin for just a few neurons. Perhaps there was a bit of her brain that was calm, but she couldn't find it, the chocolate didn't find it and the chamomile got lost somewhere in the chaos Joli was hiding within her. The journey was long and hard. It didn't get easier. If Joli would have eaten her body weight in dark chocolate, it probably wouldn't have made any difference. Joli and all her need for calm were on the platform in Westfront, Kyle walking towards all of it. The thing was Kyle had brought his own share of unmanageability and powerlessness, things he'd learnt about at rehab. Things he couldn't bloody cope with at the moment.

There was just enough room in Kyle's car for the two of them and all of their stress and unmanageability. Kyle, totally wired, carefully drove them back to his flat. They got inside and Kyle could hear the gear screaming from the bathroom.

Joli was sure she could hear it too. How could they be in the flat this evening and not go crazy? The truth they were both starting to realise was, they liked the crazy, the chaotic thoughts, the overpowering feelings, the buzz; this was what they wanted. They just had to learn to tame it, not get overtaken by it, overwhelmed by it, overpowered by it; no, this was to be understood, to be moulded, to be enjoyed and savoured. They talked and talked, but it wasn't two-way conversation; it was more like excited outpourings aimed at each other, all the things they wanted to say, needed to say, just flying out of their mouths, no listening, no time to think, just an explosion of everything from the last few weeks. Kyle dragged himself away from the drama for enough time to put two ready meals in the microwave, sausage and mash for two. Joli slowed herself down sufficiently to offer to go and get wine to go with dinner. Kyle gave directions to the off licence and Joli went to get a bottle of Rioja. The perfect accompaniment to sausage and mash.

They sat for dinner and wine, a moment of calm, they got their breath back as they dined on the finest of ready meals; at least the wine was decent. Kyle mentioned the gear and how it was pulling him to use it again. He thought about the words to kill again, but he didn't like that way of describing what he was doing; it wasn't killing, it was just supported overdose. Whatever, he wanted to do it again. Joli wanted to be involved, to kill, she cared less about the terminology — it was the doing she wanted, the game; it was a game for her. She hoped it would be, but she hadn't started playing yet, she wanted to start, but they had to talk, they had to plan and they had to make some rules to their game, otherwise it would get sloppy and they'd risk getting caught and that would ruin the game, where was the fun in prison?

They talked into the night, discussing their next moves. Kyle felt he would be safer if he kept out of Cornwall and he suggested he should go to Plymouth for his next act. Joli felt she was OK in Cornwall but maybe needed to make her appearance seem a little less obvious. They had enough gear for them both to make up two hits, but to not use one. As they planned the adrenalin rushed through their bodies, they broke off from planning for sex, but it was the planning they wanted; the synergy between them was electric as they plotted and schemed, it seemed to dissipate during the physicality of sex. They were locked in an embrace of thinking and imagining, but the details were starting to crystallise into the semblance of a plan. They were working together but apart, independent individuals with a common goal. Nothing more to do today, they went to bed, to dream about the things to come. Disturbed sleep, as their subconscious minds collided throughout the night.

NA Meetings

Lucy clattered around her cottage, banging into things loudly, clumsily moving from room to room, hiding her crossness from nobody, especially herself, as she was thinking about which dress to wear. Unfortunately, it wasn't for the romantic liaison with Shona she'd been looking forward to, but to the NA meeting. If she couldn't wear the dress for her date, she could wear it to share about why she wasn't having a bloody date. Shona hadn't contacted her, she wasn't here and that was enough. Shona had ignored Lucy's texts and calls and it seemed obvious she was somewhere else, and more than likely with someone else.

Lucy tried not to care, but she did care, she remembered those first flutters of excitement she'd felt with Shona, the anticipation of time together, intimate time sharing each other. Lucy wasn't going to be sharing anything with Shona; the only share was going to be at NA. Lucy laid the flowery dress on the bed, the flowery one, that was the one, the little black number was too revealing for NA. She didn't exactly know the NA crowd yet, and she didn't want them thinking she was only there on the pull; she so definitely wasn't. She was making a statement to herself, she could wear her dress when she wanted, for herself, not for other people. Recovery was about her, and how she felt. There it was, that empowered woman, who'd been hiding within her; she was here now, expressing herself in what she was going to wear. She stopped and thought, it's just a bloody dress, not a political statement of intent, but it did seem important.

Lucy left the dress and its political importance on the bed and went for a walk along the front, to clear her mind and to listen to the sea. It sounded different to the sea in Brighton. Somehow it was less frenetic, gentler, maybe less going on. Certainly, less background noise, less traffic, less industry, apart from fishing and tourism. Lucy hadn't heard any industry. Cornwall itself was calmer than Brighton, by the sea and everywhere else. Lucy liked it, as she wandered along the front listening to the gulls overhead and watching the boats bobbing around in the harbour. A few people sailing in dinghies, and on paddle boards, enjoying the autumn evening sun, but generally pretty deserted; another quiet day in Cornwall. The gentle lapping of the sea, the pulling of the waves against the stony sand and the power of the ocean as it just relentlessly does its thing, satisfyingly permanent, always there, always being, consistent, dependable. Some of the qualities she wanted in her life, the things that have been missing since she met Nate, but really it started before that, when she was a teenager; that's when it started to go wrong, when she had to be all that she needed. Lucy thought about what she needed now, someone to lean on, someone strong, someone who cared for her, someone she hadn't met yet. Lucy took in the sounds of the sea as she wandered home. It was great to live this close to the ocean, especially now the weather was so pleasant, perhaps the winter would be more of a drag?

Lucy cleared up after tea and started getting ready for the meeting. This was proper getting ready, not just throwing on some clothes. Getting ready like it was a date. The significance of it was important to Lucy. She wanted to put it all behind her, let go of the resentments as she let go of Shona. She didn't want to carry that relationship baggage any more, she didn't want to carry any baggage. Now it was all about living in the moment, and one day at a time and all the mindfulness clichés she could think of. It would be if that worked, but it was so hard; she just wanted to scream out loud, something about a bitch and selfishness and dying. Not very kind, or forgiving, not very accepting and certainly not what recovery was about. That was all OK in theory, but now this was real and being angry was OK, but how do you let go of angry when there's so much of it? Getting ready to go was taking a long time, being angry wasn't helping. Putting on the dress hadn't helped. This wasn't what the dress was for; she was supposed to be having fun in this dress, taking risks, not sharing her bloody heartache in this dress.

Kyle drove to Plymouth. There was a meeting just outside the centre of Plymouth. He was just going to see, he'd not been to Plymouth NA before, so this was just a chance to get a picture of the people and see who was there. If he was lucky, the right person might be there, but he wasn't going to take a chance, not after their planning session. Joli was going to a meeting he knew, but she'd not been, so she had to remain in the background, not attract attention. That was the problem being at a meeting for the first time — people noticed, that was his worry too, Plymouth was new territory for him, could he just go in and out unnoticed?

The meeting was at a church hall, and when he got there, he could already see a few people outside chatting and smoking. They were unmistakable, the way they stood, the way they moved, how they interacted with each other, the interplay, the body language, it was so NA, so life in recovery, so obvious. Kyle knew they were his people, but not really his people. He knew he was different — he was like Joli — she was his kind of person.

Kyle chatted to the Plymouth crowd. They were just as welcoming as Cornwall and Bristol, but Kyle didn't want welcome, he wanted to be unnoticed. He tried to stay in the background of the conversation, hiding in plain sight, no comments or opinions, nothing to attract attention, could he just slide in and slide out without being noticed and even better, could he find a victim? Not yet he couldn't. It was a male only crowd at the moment, but there was still ten minutes to go; it could be a long and wasted journey if a few more people didn't turn up. They started to make their way through to the hall and a few more people tagged onto the group, two women walked in, but they weren't the vulnerable waifs Kyle was looking for, these were robust women who definitely didn't give off the message of neediness.

The meeting started and Kyle had already stopped listening, NA person sharing the same old thing about the same old life involving the same old people. Where was the originality in any of it? Did people really life lives like this? And if they did, why, oh why, would they bother to tell other people about it? Surely this was just some strange game that was being played out in front of him, that he didn't understand or know about. Some game of competitive boredom, some low stakes poker, had he really wasted his evening for this? He looked around the room, hoping he might have missed someone with his earlier scan. He hadn't, this actually was it, this evening, he was going to be in the presence of share after share of escalating dullness, no excitement, no thrill, no high, just a wasted trip.

Ninety minutes is a long time, Kyle thought to himself. Not one person worth hearing, not a clue as to if there ever would be. Kyle didn't want to ask, for the risk of attention; slide in, slide out, that was the plan. He'd try a different night and venue next week and hope for a better turnout. He looked around the room; it couldn't be worse, he thought. It wasn't that he didn't like any of these people, it was that he just didn't care about any of them. If only they would just shut up and then he could go home. Mel was the last to speak, she started her share, she looked so angry, her face twisted and contorted as she talked about her ex and how he stopped her from seeing her daughter again today, another day, a different excuse, but the same outcome, for her. Lost and helpless, desperate to be the mum she was before the drugs took over, but now, now she was clean why wasn't everything working out like it should? Why wouldn't he let her be that mum, why the hatred, and why did it make her so angry and so sad at the same time? The tears were rolling down her face as she talked about her cravings and fighting off the urge to use, how being in recovery for years didn't make it easier and the heartbreak, the sense of defeat; Kyle was listening now. The meeting was finished, and everyone just seemed to mingle and chat. Kyle moved to the edge, he wanted to speak to Mel privately and he wanted to speak urgently, he didn't want to lose the moment.

Mel moved through the people and was alongside Kyle. Kyle looked at Mel and put his arms out to hug her. She opened hers and they hugged., Kyle said gently, through using his vulnerable voice, "That was some share, Mel. I don't know how you feel, because I can't, but I'm going through the same with my Beth, I've not seen her for three years."

Mel was looking at Kyle now, tears still in her eyes. "Let's go somewhere and talk, Kyle." And with that they walked out the hall.

Mel knew a café they could go to that would still be open, or they could go to a pub? Mel didn't mind pubs. Heroin had always been her thing, not alcohol. Kyle didn't mind, he admitted to still having a drink. It was heroin for him too, but he was driving, so coffee was better; he found going into a pub and not drinking, strange at least, but also really difficult. They settled on a café and ordered a couple of coffees and some toast and jam.

Mel just looked broken; however, she mustered some energy to ask Kyle about his daughter. "Kyle, tell me about Beth?" she said, in an almost apologetic manner.

Kyle didn't look up and started to mutter. "Me and Jen never married, we did a lot of gear together, we lived in Bristol, she's moved now, I don't know where. When she got pregnant, she cleaned up, she didn't mind me still using, just not at home. But when Beth was born, she just changed. I wasn't allowed near her or the baby. I never got the chance to get clean. It seemed to just sneak up on me, and she never said, she just changed. Then she left, with Beth, when Beth was about two months. I tried to get clean, but I never managed it for long enough. I last saw Jen and Beth about three years ago. Beth was two. And I screwed up and turned up wasted for a birthday party. Jen and her family never forgave me. Jen's moved away, and her parents won't talk to me. It was my fault, but I'm clean now and I don't think I'll ever get to be a dad again."

Mel was crying and reached over the table to hold Kyle's hand, with both her hands, she looked into Kyle's eyes, straight into his best vulnerable look and said, "That's so sad, Kyle, what are you going to do? What are we going to do?"

Kyle held her gaze, and then looked down again. He knew that looking down and talking quietly gave the right impression. "I don't know what to do, I just keep going, but every now and then it just hurts. Your share, well it hit a nerve and made me feel raw. But what about you, your ex knocked you back today, that's really hard."

Mel cried again, sobbing at the thought of not seeing her daughter. "April, my daughter's called April. She was four in April; she needs her mum. I'm allowed to see her, but Tony, he just keeps changing the rules, because he sees me as an addict, a waster, he doesn't want her near his precious daughter. His family are the same and I'm just on the outside being pushed further away."

They shared more stories of not seeing their daughters and how their manipulative partners constantly kept changing the rules and letting them down. They drank coffee and ate toast as they bonded over their mutual heartbreak, Mel's real, Kyle's invented, purely for the sport of Kyle manipulating Mel some more. Mel asked Kyle if he wanted to get together again, maybe go for a late lunch tomorrow at the Barbican. Although she'd cried throughout their time together, he'd listened and supported and said the right words at the right time and Mel hadn't had that for a while, she'd missed it. She felt that for once someone actually cared, someone liked her and didn't talk over her or down to her, someone actually took the time to try and understand her, and that someone was worth seeing again.

Lunch plans were made, and Kyle offered to give Mel a lift home. She didn't need one, she nearly was home. They walked out of the café and up the hill a few hundred yards, then Mel turned left, stopped and turned to Kyle. "This is me, thanks for walking me home, see you tomorrow," and she looked up and kissed him on the cheek, more a peck than a kiss. Kyle didn't look away, he smiled as he looked in Mel's eyes. Then they kissed again, this time a long kiss. Mel's lips were wet through crying, but she felt some excitement in the kiss. There hadn't been much of that in her life this last year. "Do you want to come in, Kyle?"

Kyle tried to put his sexy look on, he wasn't sure if he had one. "No Mel, not tonight, I'll see you for lunch, tomorrow afternoon." They kissed again and then Kyle was walking back to his car, over his shoulder he said, "Night Mel."

She replied, "See you tomorrow, Kyle, goodnight."

Westfront NA didn't normally have people dressing to attend, but tonight it did; Lucy looked stunning. The regulars who were standing around outside, smoking and chatting all stopped and stared. One of them said he was sorry for staring, but did she know how gorgeous she looked, and did she know this was just an NA meeting? Lucy replied, "Yes I know, oops, no I didn't know I was gorgeous and yes, I do know it's NA. There's a reason, you'll hear." The guys crowded around Lucy, chatting, being friendly and looking, more looking than chatting, really. NA wasn't the place for women to go all dressed up, well not normally in Westfront. Joli walked past the group of men surrounding Lucy and into the meeting, almost unnoticed, a baseball cap covering her hair and jeans, trainers and a fleece, hiding most of her skin, no makeup to attract any attention, just Joli doing her best to blend and look ordinary.

The meeting was quite busy, lively, almost vibrant, and Lucy contributed significantly to that vibe. She was almost the star attraction, Lucy thought; men can be so shallow and easily pleased, a pretty girl in a dress and that's it for most of them. The meeting started as normal with a couple of shares that were neither brief nor interesting, but people need to offload because it works. Lucy stood up and at that stage you could've heard a pin drop, everyone wanted to know more. Lucy explained that she'd bought the dress for a date, a first date, but the person had let her down, she hadn't even told her it was off, she'd just left her with no one to wear it for. So, she wore the dress to NA to get rid of the resentments that were building up inside her, the anger boiling inside, she wanted to swear but today she was being ladylike, dressed up and proper, inside she was furious, and hurting. She hadn't relapsed, although that was more by luck than anything else, she wanted to drink, she wanted to get off her face on heroin, she wanted it to all go away, to stop hurting, to stop feeling, to just be calm inside.

Lucy thanked her sponsor for all her support and everyone tonight for being lovely. She sat down. The meeting seemed to stall, the atmosphere had been intense throughout her share; she spoke in a captivating, gentle way, pulling people in as she described her emotional instability, her problems of controlling her inner addict and how bloody difficult life can be. There were a couple more shares, but the meeting was over really. No one's share got past Lucy's; she had reluctantly retained her celebrity status.

After the meeting it was Lucy this and Lucy that, not what Lucy wanted but people in early recovery can be insensitive too, and Lucy was trying to get away. Joli sensed this and whispered in Lucy's ear. "Can we go somewhere quiet and talk?"

Lucy turned and for the first time that night, someone noticed Joli's smile and eyes. "Yes, I'd like that," said Lucy.

They walked out together, no one actually noticing who Lucy was with, exactly how Joli had planned it. They walked and found a high street coffee shop open until late, they went to the counter, ordered coffees and then went to the back and sat down. Joli smiled. "You do look amazing, Lucy." A coy, embarrassed look and Lucy managed a "thanks". Joli looked questioningly at Lucy. "Can I tell you why I had to talk to you tonight?" Lucy nodded.

Joli steeled herself, making it look as if a big thing was about to be said.

"Your share tonight just spoke to me. I felt for you every second that you were speaking. She just treated you so badly; I loved it that you wore the dress you bought for the date and shared about it. I hope it helped."

Lucy shook her head. "I don't think it did."

Then Joli carried on. "Last week I was supposed to go to a family wedding with my girlfriend, Sue. We didn't go. It was the first time we were going to be a couple in front of her family, nine months we'd been together, her flat, my flat, we virtually lived together. It was her cousin's wedding. I didn't know them, I never met her family, I never will now. She went with a man from work, someone she barely knew. She'd rather be seen with a man she barely knew than me, her girlfriend. I was devastated, I came down here to stay with a friend, to get away from Bristol and all her stuff, all her memories, hiding in my flat, in my life, but not in Westfront." Joli didn't know how to cry, she hesitated and stuttered a couple of times, pretending to force out the lies, but they fell so easily from her tongue.

Joli looked across at Lucy and with a cheeky look across her face said, “So here I am, single in Westfront, looking for a beautiful girl and something to do. What do you think my chances are?”

Lucy smiled. “Well, apparently I look amazing, and I’m looking for something to do.”

Joli liked that, and she did look amazing. Joli thought for a minute and said, “Maybe I could take you out to dinner tomorrow, we could both dress for a date, what do you think?”

Lucy blushed. “I think we should definitely go on a date tomorrow, where should we go?” They flirted with each other for a few more minutes, with lots of touching and giggling, a little bit more touching and just a bit of kissing and somehow throughout all of that they made a plan for tomorrow. Lucy smiled inside and couldn’t help but say, “The dress worked, it was for a date. I can call this a date, can’t I?”

Joli leant across so her face was close to Lucy’s and she softly said, “I’d like you to call it a date,” and they kissed again.

They left the café and walked back to where Lucy’s car was parked. They stopped and held hands, looking at each other. Lucy wanted to say everything, she’d been dreading this evening, sharing at NA, everyone looking at her, being the centre of all that attention, leaving the meeting on her own, feeling lonely, feeling sad, feeling all those horrible feelings that she hadn’t wanted to feel. Instead, she felt empowered, she’d had a good evening, she’d felt special, she’d been heard, she’d been noticed, and she’d actually had a good time.

Flirting was always fun, kissing and touching was great, but it was the anticipation she hadn't expected, the looking forward to tomorrow, the flip in her stomach, the tingle on her skin, the dryness in her mouth. She didn't say all that, though, she just said, "Thanks for this evening, see you tomorrow."

Joli hadn't said a lot of things either, but her feelings were slightly different, the lies, the control, the manipulation, the game, it was all playing out so beautifully. Lucy, so pathetic, so easy, so much fun. Joli escaped from her scheming mind. "Tomorrow then, it's a date." They kissed and Joli turned and walked off back towards Kyle's place.

Joli didn't expect Kyle to be back from Plymouth. She knew it was a couple of hours' drive and, the meeting didn't finish until nine. Even if he left as soon as it finished, she'd still beat him back to the flat. As it was, she had a key and she just wanted to sleep, playing Lucy had been tiring. She'd text him when she got into bed, she could gloat and brag tomorrow, unless of course, Kyle had something to brag about tonight? Joli got into bed, she sent Kyle a text, just saying goodnight and that she was tired. She was asleep within seconds.

Kyle was making breakfast when Joli woke up. "Breakfast in bed, kisses for me," she sleepily sang.

Kyle walked over and kissed her. "Morning, you gorgeous thing, do you want coffee and breakfast?"

She grabbed his hand and pulled him onto the bed. "And kisses," she said through that amazing smile. Joli sat up, naked, entirely comfortable with her body. She stood up and walked towards the kitchen, grabbed a coffee and sat down. Kyle moved closer to Joli, for some of those kisses. Joli's hands were playfully undoing Kyle's trousers as she said, "Where's my breakfast in bed?"

Kyle was soon as naked as Joli, and no longer interested in breakfast. Joli turned the rings of the cooker off and led Kyle back to bed. They were hungry for sex, but not love making; this was competition sex, almost violent, no tenderness, just each of them trying to meet their needs, not caring about the other's enjoyment. It wasn't about giving pleasure, it was about reaching climax and exploding with satisfaction. The adrenalin, the scheming, the manipulating, the lying, the thoughts of killing, the anticipation, the taking from someone, the control, using a body for pleasure, both of their spent, sweaty bodies grappling for the last ounce of pleasure to be taken, not given, nothing given, just taken and used.

Nothing was said after sex. They just grabbed some clothes and returned to the kitchen and started recooking breakfast. More coffee and then toast, to go with the bacon and eggs and soon they were sat next to each other eating and talking, still too excited to have a proper conversation, talking over each other, not taking time to listen; no highly developed interpersonal skills were being used, no attempt to understand the other person's story, no empathy, just me, me, me. They both knew they could be like this and they seemed to realise at the same time. They got up with their coffees and sat on the sofa and they both said at the same time, "You go first." Joli cupped her hands around her mug of lukewarm coffee and said, "I'll make us some hot coffee; you tell me about your day."

Kyle relayed his story from yesterday. He told Joli about Mel, the crying woman who couldn't see her daughter, he then told her about the beautiful lie he had spun to show how empathic he was, because he couldn't see his pretend daughter; then through their shared trauma they drank coffee, whilst she cried some more. He was cruel as he took delight from her heartbreak. He was meeting her for a late lunch in Plymouth and then he'd go back to her flat, for sex and heroin and then she'd be dead, after that, he'd come home. It was very matter of fact, no guilt about the plan to have sex with another woman and no guilt associated with the lifeforce he was planning to extinguish. Kyle didn't do guilt, or he hadn't so far, no guilt, no remorse, no sorrow, just conquest. Kyle liked conquest; he certainly knew what that felt like. Joli had made the coffee, and sat, looking longingly at Kyle, loving the story of control and the deviousness of the lie, the game of it all. Joli so loved the game, she never asked about Mel. The crying woman's fate didn't bother Joli; she was just nothing, no one, the thought of her being dead, that was what Joli loved, that beautiful thought, dancing around inside her head.

"My go now," Joli blurted out. Joli told Kyle about Lucy and how pathetic she was in her dress, after being stood up by her girlfriend. How she whined and whinged and then Joli's wonderful lie about her ex-girlfriend ditching her so she could take a man to a family wedding. They went for coffee and flirted and kissed and today she was taking her out for dinner and then she'd go back to her flat for sex and heroin and then the pathetic woman would be dead and the game would be finished for the day. Joli didn't care about the details now. Yesterday was done and today was perfectly set; the outcome wasn't certain, but it was playing out just how Joli wanted it to. Kyle wasn't sure what he felt, was it pride, was it wonder, was it love, was this what he'd been looking for all his life? A partner in crime, a partner in everything, her smile, her eyes, her wonderful lies, her delightful scheming, her utter ruthlessness, her absolute perfection. They were going to have a fantastic day.

A Double Date

As Kyle left for Plymouth, Joli was doing her makeup. She kissed him and laughed as she'd left lipstick on his lips, she wiped it off. "You'll not bed that crying woman if you've got my lipstick on." No jealousy, just enjoying the game. Kyle had deliberately underdressed, jeans, tee shirt, but his new leather jacket so it looked as if he'd made some effort. After all it was a date, and a very important one. Plymouth is a fairly easy drive, but not one that Kyle could do every day. After this, he was planning a few days' rest, no pressure, just feet up and maybe the odd movie, some down time with Joli, no plans. Kyle was driving at Goldilocks' pace, not too fast, not too slow, just the right speed. He didn't want to attract attention, he didn't want to be late either; Mel might not wait. He was pretty sure she would, but he wasn't taking any chances. With the Coral keeping him company Kyle arrived at the Barbican. Parking had been easier than he'd expected, and Kyle was soon walking through the cobbled streets of the Barbican, looking at the boats bobbing wealthily about in the harbour, the sun bouncing off their chrome fittings.

Mel walked up to Kyle, not disguising her delight at not being stood up. Mel had started to aim low with men and dates. Kyle was way above where her bar had previously been set, boyfriends who weren't pissed, off their heads on drugs, violent, disrespectful; the list could go on. Mel hadn't been that lucky with men over the last two years. Sex had been easy; decency was where she had struggled, hence the delight with Kyle. He seemed to tick all the boxes and even if he did drink or use occasionally, that didn't bother Mel; she kind of dabbled too. They kissed and held hands as they walked along the busy pavements, stopping and looking at the menus at each restaurant or bar as they passed, deciding on a busy, vibrant restaurant with tables overflowing into the street. They sat outside, which was a great relief to Mel, who still couldn't manage to stop smoking; she wasn't that good at stopping anything really. Soon they'd ordered wine to go with the food they couldn't decide on. Wine was easy, just pick a colour and order. Neither of them cared that much about quality, they were quantity people, today they'd chosen white and specifically a Chardonnay. Mel thought that that would probably be OK and not too expensive. The chatting was easy. Mel talking about her and Kyle just listening and asking the odd question, not probing too deep, not asking too much. Mel wanted to talk about her daughter April. Unfortunately, she was so raw inside that the mere thought of her brought tears almost instantly. At this stage, Kyle must've picked up on her emotions as he said, "Tell me about April?" Kyle had been waiting for the right moment to ask, he didn't want to appear cruel. However, he did want her to run through the emotional mill; that way it was easier for him to relate. Bigger emotions were more easily observed, and he could fake empathy more easily when he could read the feelings. Tears and heartache were easy to read.

Mel started talking about April. "Being a mum and never really understanding post-natal depression and one of my friends offered me some tablets to help me make it through the day. The tablets were OK, but I never felt right. April just seemed completely unmanageable, and needy, all day. There was no sleep and Tony didn't help, he just said it was my job, because he had to be up for work and then at the weekends he went out with his friends. I was just at home, with April, I was a wreck, no sleep, I couldn't think straight, the tablets were a help and then one day I got offered some heroin. To be honest at the time I'd have said yes to anything, but that first hit, I felt so good, even though I was as sick as a dog after I didn't care, I just wanted more. My new friends accepted me, well they accepted April as well, they seemed to like having a baby around; it was a bit of novelty. I never felt she was in any danger. She was in a pram; there's no way a needle could have hurt her. I didn't have much that was worth stealing, so it just felt safe, me and my baby, in a drug den. Tony didn't see it the same as me, when he found us that day. He still can't talk about it today, where I'd taken his baby, what I'd become, some drug whore, well I think that's what he called me, what his mum has called me a few times. That hurts, when I think about how much I wanted to impress her when we first dated. I went from that nice young girl dating her precious son to that drug whore who was never going to see April again."

Kyle leant over and touched her arm, to try to calm her, "I think our food's coming, are you going to be all right?"

Mel looked up, smiling, teary eyes. She seemed grateful. "Yes, it's good to talk, let's drink and eat."

They clinked glasses and appreciated the plates of food that were set before them. The food looked great. Mel couldn't see it, but her mouth was watering, and the different scents excited her palate as she prepared to eat, not knowing where to start. Kyle wasn't too bothered, he wasn't exactly thinking about the food, he had bigger things to be focussing his senses on. The food would do, the wine was all right, the day was going to plan. The heroin was screaming at him. Keeping it quiet, ignoring its calling, he started eating his beef, always the meat first, that's the best part, the point of the meal. Mel was getting her composure back, so Kyle applied the pressure again. "So, what happened when he found you both, that day?"

Mel looked wounded, as though the very idea of that day could cut her insides open. "He grabbed April and left, he went to his mum's, he didn't say anything. I didn't know what to do, I was an addict now, I was using sixty to seventy pounds of gear a day, I couldn't stop. I didn't even go after him, I thought it would be all right by the time I got home. It wasn't, it wasn't all right ever again. I tried to quit, I didn't know how to, and then the pain got so much, the emotions, him, his family, April, I just couldn't cope, but heroin, it made everything go away. So I was stuck for about two years, in some sort of using limbo, no life, and then NA, I got clean, but that was it, nothing else changed, the people in my life, my life, it didn't get better. I just had all the pain with nothing to take it away. So, I get pissed occasionally and make poor choices about who I sleep with, and then I go to NA and share, and I cry a lot."

Kyle had just about finished his dinner and he wanted more wine. "Mel, are you ready for some more wine?"

Mel smiled, no tears. "Always," she said as she started tucking into her dinner. Mel was enjoying the meal, the wine and the company. Kyle was easy on the eye, he listened when she spoke and he paid attention, to the little things, the details; she liked him, she was definitely going to enjoy more of him later. As Mel enjoyed her wine she sat back and looked longingly at Kyle. He was certainly a better grade boyfriend than the normal low life she let into her bed. He was quite a catch; she was definitely feeling that she'd got a result today, was getting a result, was having a result. She wanted to enjoy every moment of being with Kyle and she wanted to take him home now. "Kyle, let's go back to my place. I want you. I want you now, here, but I can wait till we get back to my place."

Kyle was sold on the idea. "I want you too, I'll have to leave my car here, though, we'll need to get a taxi."

Mel's flat was quite spacious and looked larger than it was due to minimal furniture and nothing but bare walls and blinds against the windows. No pictures, no ornaments, no photos, nothing apart from a table and chairs, a sofa, and a bed and a chest of drawers. Kyle was fine with that; all he needed was a bed and maybe another bottle of wine. Mel found a bottle of wine in the fridge and glasses in the cupboard. She poured them both a generous home measure of wine and handed one to Kyle. They clinked glasses and moved to the sofa. Mel moved close to Kyle and started undoing his belt, she wanted him undressed now. She wanted more wine; she emptied her glass and went to the fridge to quickly refill both glasses; that was the bottle gone. Before she sat down, she took off her dress and sat down in just her bra and knickers, happy with her body. She pulled Kyle's trousers off and then his shirt. They stood up and finished undressing each other as they made their way to bed, clothes strewn over the living room floor.

As they landed on the bed Kyle said, "Sex and heroin."

Mel laughed. "Have you got gear?"

Kyle touched and talked. "It's for afters."

Mel touched and smiled. "I can wait, for gear, not for sex." They writhed around on the bed, together, sex, what they wanted, needed, their bodies lost in each other, Kyle thinking more about after sex than sex, but present enough for Mel not to notice. Sex was great, well it was for Mel, Kyle had been attentive, gentle and all the things Mel wanted of someone to share with, not pissed, not violent, not everyone else she'd had sex with this year. This was what she wanted, but now she wanted heroin. The desire never went away. Now it was clinging to her, filling her life full of wanting, what was he doing, why was it taking so long? She could hear the veins in arms screaming for heroin, it was ages since the last time. She had to have it now, what was he doing? Kyle handed her the needle, she tried not to snatch it from him or scream what took you so long, the vein screamed for her, she injected, and then just seemed to fall slowly forwards. Kyle watched and waited.

Joli got out of the taxi at the bank, by the bottom of town, looking around for Lucy. She saw a very sexy looking woman in an amazing black dress. Wherever they went they were going to attract attention. Joli looked pretty stunning in her black dress, red shoes and red jacket. They walked towards each other and kissed, held hands and looked each other up and down, appraising each other. This was sexual; they wanted each other. Joli smiled, her best sexy smile. "Can you wait until after dinner?"

Lucy felt that she'd been caught, being just slightly naughty. "Oh, if I have to," she playfully responded. They giggled and walked, holding hands, leaning into each other as they stumbled slightly in their heels. Thankfully, the restaurant wasn't far to walk to and they were soon sat near the back of a very nice Italian, looking at the menus and each other. Lucy steadied herself and forcefully said, “I know I’ve just come out of rehab, but this is a proper date and I want a proper drink. I want something bubbly and expensive and I don’t care what you want, I want bubbly.”

Joli giggled, “I don’t mind a bit of bubbly, and I love that sassy attitude. You have what you want, I’m going to have what I want.”

They ordered bubbly, and food, a variety of starters, a big salad, with the idea of dessert to finish the evening off. The bubbly was gone before the food arrived, and a bottle of chianti was decided on, and maybe some sparkling water to make the wine last longer. Joli asked gentle questions and Lucy opened up a little, talking about her past, the disappointments that had been her parents, the life in Brighton, her job and then her fall into drugs with Nate. Joli listened, touched, nodded and kept eye contact as long as Lucy could cope with it. Joli knew when to look away, to distract herself. Lucy asked about Joli’s past and Joli happily shared about her lost job and the drug binge that followed and then rehab. Joli then talked about imaginary girlfriends, annoying boyfriends and then her recent partner who ditched her a couple of weeks ago. Lucy was drunk, trying to listen, but not really capable, interested but not retaining things; the bubbly had gone straight to her head. “I think I need some coffee and cake, before I take you back to my place.” The waiter must’ve been in earshot as he was there instantly, taking their order and clearing some space for their desserts as well as ordering their taxi.

Dessert was lovely, sweet and full of flavour, but Lucy wanted to go now, she wanted Joli, she was drunk, she was full, but she was far from satisfied; what little focus she had left, was focussed entirely on Joli — she had an amazing smile, she just looked so good. Lucy slurred, “Let’s go, Joli, I’ve had enough.”

Joli was warming up. “I’ve only just got started, Lucy. We’ll finish off at your place.” Joli paid for dinner, she’d taken cash out earlier as she didn’t want a trail of where they’d been. The taxi arrived and dropped them off on the front, near Lucy’s, but a few minutes’ walk away. Joli had said she wanted to walk off the dinner and get some air. Lucy needed some air too; she was starting to get nervous. All the wanting wasn’t the same as doing, and she’d never had sex with a woman before. Joli held her hand and seemed to sense Lucy’s anxiety. They arrived at Lucy’s front door, and Joli was all hands whilst Lucy fumbled with the key. Inside the cottage Lucy relaxed, she felt more in control, she pulled Joli in and kissed her, and started to undress her, the lyrics of Mr Brightside in her head, takes off her dress now. Joli in her lingerie looked fantastic; Lucy was helped out of her dress, feeling conscious of her body but Joli touched and kissed as they made their way upstairs to bed, drunken fumblings and they were both naked, Joli in control and Lucy’s nerves completely gone as she was lost in the discovery and wonder that was Joli; her tenderness and sensuousness was blissful, but, and there was a but — something was missing. Joli felt it too — something was missing, and Joli said, “Sex and heroin.”

Lucy hadn’t thought that heroin was missing but now it had been mentioned it most certainly was missing. “Have you got some?”

“Of course, I have, sex and heroin, what else could we have?”

“Where is it? Get it now. I want it.”

"I'm getting it, it's in my bag." If Lucy had ever wanted anything more in her life she couldn't remember. The wine was gone, the heroin wasn't ready, what was she supposed to do?

After waiting for what seemed like hours, her aching, craving body, writhed on the bed, where was she? Joli walked back into the room and Lucy had time to admire her naked body before her gaze was drawn to the needle, her outstretched arm, desperate for the fix, her body empty, ready. The vein, impatiently prepared and Lucy injected, she just seemed to stop. Everything about her was different; she was no longer craving, she was spent.

Kyle looked at Mel. She was still breathing, lying on her side, looking up, not yet coming around. Kyle hadn't planned this, he sat next to her on the bed, thinking that this was wrong — she was supposed to be dead, she should be dead, why was she still alive? The last few days were about dying, not about surviving, not about coming around; it was supposed to be overdose and finished. The pillow was in his hands. Not thinking, he turned it around in his hands, then he held it over her face, pressing it against her mouth and nose, before she had chance to catch her breath it was taken from her, the pillow held firm against her face. She didn't struggle, she just stopped trying and then she was gone. Kyle stood up and looked at the lifeless body of Mel, what had he done? He'd just killed her. He needed to make it look as if she'd overdosed and just smothered herself. If he put her on her front and just left, he thought he'd be all right.

He started to get dressed but he wasn't really thinking. The blood was rushing through his body, the adrenalin, the excitement, the rush, the murder, what had he done, but how did it feel? His phone was ringing. He checked the screen — it was Joli. Kyle answered. “Hi Joli, you won’t believe what’s happened,” but Joli didn’t say anything. It was Train playing down the phone, “Drops of Jupiter” and with the phone to his ear, Kyle started to dance around the room, and as he twirled, and spun to Train, he could hear laughing and dancing in the background.